T0128133

Incoming

Incoming
Collected Stories

VIC AMATO

INCOMING
COLLECTED STORIES

This is a work of fiction. All of the characters, names, incidents,
organizations, and dialogue in these stories are either the products
of the author's imagination or are used fictitiously.

iUniverse books may be ordered through booksellers or by contacting:

iUniverse
1663 Liberty Drive
Bloomington, IN 47403
www.iuniverse.com
1-800-Authors (1-800-288-4677)

Three of the stories have appeared elsewhere in slightly different
form-- "Second Person '67" in Short Stories Bi-Monthly;
"Rex Sivle Declines" in Catch-Up and "Who Ripped Off My
Lunch" in Watermark. All rights retained by the author.

ISBN: 978-1-4917-6239-4 (sc)
ISBN: 978-1-4917-6240-0 (e)
Library of Congress Control Number: 2015904648

Print information available on the last page.

iUniverse rev. date: 04/13/2015

For Susan Elinor

Contents

Death by Peanut Butter

"HAPPY NEW YEAR. HEY. TWAIN DIED." JANET, MY executive director, stuck her head in my door and gave me the news. Her head was at a slight angle, and her dark hair fell away from her face on the side away from me.

"Did he fall off the riverboat?" I had just sat down at my desk with my coffee after being off for nine days during the holidays.

"Ha ha. Check it out. It should be in there." She stepped in, nodded her head and long neck toward the foot-high stack of papers filling my inbox, and then went on down the hall.

"Happy New Year to you too." I'm not sure she heard me.

After digging through the pile, I learned from the incident report that Twain, a (mental health) consumer, whose incidents I had investigated previously, had suffered a heart attack and had expired on his group home driveway. He was ailing—living on borrowed time for some time—and lucky to reach seventy-nine. He was our oldest ambulatory residential consumer.

He departed this life on December 26, what they call Boxing Day in Canada, now more than a week ago. Already buried. Adult Protective Services passed on investigating his death, and the Sheriff's Department and EMS did the minimum. Their reports, which I had faxed to me, provided little additional information.

The consumer, who had become known in these parts as Twain, was as crazy as a jaybird, to use an unprofessional but fitting term. We, Community Mental Health, got him because Port Huron, Michigan, is the end of the line. Both I-94 and I-69 terminate at the Blue Water Bridge. You can't walk across the bridge anymore because of the high cost of retrieving jumper suicides, which can be as much as $50,000 for the marine patrol and scuba divers to search in the strong current of the St. Clair River. Twain was headed for Toronto but didn't get all the way over to Canadian customs, where he would have needed a passport. As a pedestrian, he was halted on the US side and found to have no ID whatsoever. When questioned, he claimed, "The Devil is after me," and presented himself as a clinically confused person. The border guys called the county sheriff, and after a short interview at the jail, the deputies called us. The criminal justice system could not be applied to him by way of fingerprints or other records, and the sheriff was only too glad to pass on a mental case.

Twain, polite and mannerly, said he had hitchhiked up to the bridge. Considering his intellectual deficit, it's more likely a caretaker dumped him off. He had a mouse under his right eye. We checked with Amtrak, which also ends in Port Huron, but they, too, knew nothing of him. He told us his age but wouldn't give any more personal information. Somewhat later, he let it slip that he was familiar with Saint Louis, but that wasn't enough for us to send him back there. (Missouri couldn't help us identify him.) Thin and moderately tall, Twain, as in Mark Twain, was the name the staff picked for him for no other reasons than the Mississippi connection and that he had a large stock of fluffy white hair.

"I like that name," he said. In another a weak moment, he told a fellow consumer that his name might have been John, but now he would rather be called by his new name. Consumers have the right to be called the name of their choice, as long as it's not profane or otherwise inappropriate. So the name stuck.

We first put him in an independent studio apartment, where staff visited him each weekday to see that he was eating and cleaning up. After a fortnight or so, he spent a weekend peeling off all the wallpaper in both rooms and knocking big holes here and there. He told our staff on Monday that he'd had to drive out the demons from behind the walls. He was hospitalized, and the landlord told us he would not take him back. The landlord also put the word out to our other landlords, and Twain was blacklisted. Although he stabilized, we had no choice but to put him in a group home, where we paid for supervision.

I was involved because I'm a psychologist with Community Mental Health and I do special investigations for the Behavioral Management and Adverse Incidents Committee, which reviews major consumer incidents and deaths.

Twain's group home was designed for semi-independent consumers who still needed some daily care and help with meals and medications. Most of the residents had jobs supported by agencies for the mentally ill or mentally handicapped. Twain didn't work because he was old enough to be retired from anything disagreeable, such as working, but he went on outings with the group.

The precipitating incident occurred at lunchtime. All six residents were home. The lone staff person there had been hired the previous week. She was actually a cool-headed worker for group home personnel; she was tall and confident and in her late twenties. She had some community college education under her belt. The regular staff were, like me, taking the week off, exercising their seniority. Newbies were working throughout our system.

Twain had kind of a dry mouth, and he was unmotivated in all things, including chewing. Also, his left hand was weak, the result of an old injury or small stroke. So the standing instructions were to cut up his food. This went double for peanut butter sandwiches.

There was a new consumer in the home, Randy, who didn't belong there. Medium sized, receding brown hair, a former architect's drafter, he had hit rock bottom because of addiction to alcohol and drugs. Rehab had dried him out, but he still had bouts of deep depression. In the community, he couldn't muster enough energy to take care of himself, and the court ordered him into the mental health system. When up and functioning, he was the home's resident wiseass and know-it-all.

For lunch, Elaine, the new staff member, served up peanut butter sandwiches, chunky vegetable soup, potato chips, and a bowl of pineapple chunks. Any of these things might have choked Twain in short order, but she served it all normally because no one had told her of Twain's needs. She told me that when she set the plate down in front of Twain, he stared at it as if he'd never seen a plate of food before.

It was Randy who spoke up. "No. No, Twain needs to have his food pieced out. They never give him a whole peanut butter sandwich. He doesn't chew it good and has trouble swallowing. And he can't have chips at all. You have to watch him eat."

Elaine, not confident in Randy's veracity, processed this slowly. She decided to ask Judy, another consumer, if this was true, bypassing Twain, whom she mistrusted because he had not spoken up for himself.

Judy bobbed her head up and down. "That's what they do. Randy is right."

Elaine looked at Twain and started toward him.

"They have to cut it all up, like he was a little girl," Randy said. "He has to have little baby pieces."

Probably not enjoying being treated as a child, Twain grabbed the peanut butter sandwich, which was in whole white bread slices, not even split into halves, and stuffed it all in his mouth. He had everyone's attention, and in a second or two, he mumbled something and started to choke. Elaine grabbed his cheeks and told him to spit it out. Randy jumped up to help, and they were soon both holding Twain's head. Twain started grunting and squealing. With arms flailing, he struggled and slipped loose, knocking over everyone's beverages on the table. Then he made a break for it, opening the kitchen door and running out to the garage. Elaine and Randy pursued. The garage door was up, and Twain got as far as the snow-covered driveway before Randy grabbed him by the arm. Twain proceeded to choke and puke up most of the peanut butter sandwich and whatever else was in his stomach, much of it bursting out of his nose. Then he clutched his chest, stood up straight, twisted, and collapsed.

He lay sprawled on the driveway, not moving. Randy asked Elaine if he should perform CPR, which he knew from somewhere. She hadn't had the training, so she told him to go ahead, while she called 911. Randy pumped on Twain's chest for the entire nine minutes it took EMS to get there. The EMS guys said that some of Twain's brittle ribs had been cracked by Randy's CPR, but they added that Twain probably was dead when he hit the pavement. They did their thing, but there was never any pulse, and Twain was officially pronounced dead at the hospital, which was just a few miles away.

Yes, staff had no training, but it was the holidays. Every service entity goes bare bones at that time of year.

It was one of those things. The orders to cut up Twain's food were not written anywhere. They were not in his treatment plan, where they should have been. If no one had made a big deal out of the sandwich not being cut up, Twain probably would have eaten it in small enough bites and lived to watch Oprah that afternoon. Stuffing it in his mouth was his decision.

I cited the home for having an untrained staff person on duty alone and not having a cut–up–the–food order in his treatment plan. I required them to have Elaine fully trained as soon as possible, and have all home workers in–serviced on providing input (e.g., cutting up food) into treatment plans. Big Bill, the group home corporation executive director with whom I have had previous disagreements, complained to CEO Janet (my boss) that I was being a hard–ass and setting up his corporation for a lawsuit. To her credit, she didn't ask me to alter my findings.

Of course, I explained to her that litigation was improbable. The consumer had no guardian, and we knew of no relatives. Also, as an ancient, apartment-wrecking, demon–shadowed, troublesome mental health consumer, he likely would have been disowned long ago by his relatives, if any were living.

During the next few months, Randy progressively recovered to the point of getting his old job back in the architect's office. He left our residential system and came in only for outpatient counseling. Later, girlfriend in tow, he left the state for another job in the Chicago area, and was still there, last I heard.

The Behavioral Management and Adverse Incidents Committee accepted my report. The chief psychiatrist said Twain's death was unfortunate. Other committee members agreed. Twain had never given us his surname and so was buried as a John Doe. I reported the event on the state quarterly forms, checking boxes for "death by natural causes," "heart attack," and "while under supervision." There wasn't a box for what actually happened.

Dad List

SITTING IN THE BACK OF AN ANN ARBOR DELI, MATT bit into a hot pastrami Reuben sandwich. *Spicy and crunchy.* Just like he remembered. It was twenty past noon, and he was eating because he had given up on Jason, his son, meeting him there. Early this morning, he had e-mailed Jason at his work URL in AA on the slight chance they could meet for lunch. Matt was filling in for a sick-at-the-last-minute colleague at a one o'clock business meeting, driving down two hours.

But, oh, ye of little faith, here was Jason, funneling down the narrow path between the high brick wall and the deli counter. Tall, looking every bit an engineer with his casual shirt, pen, and mechanical pencil in his shirt pocket, Jason was clearly a career-launched man, no longer a graduate student. There was new confidence.

"Hi, Dad. Glad you started. I couldn't get away until after noon." He nodded at the pastrami as Matt was getting up. "Does that taste as good as it smells?"

"Hi, Jason." His son bent down when they hugged, Matt reaching up. "It's better. Great you could meet me. Sorry, I had to order so I can make it to my meeting." When he hugged his son, once again, it seemed so odd to him that Jason, taller since seventeen and now filled in, was so much larger than he was. *How can this be?*

"I was planning on fast food for lunch," Jason said. "This is more fun. How was your drive?"

They had a good talk. In his new phase, Jason had grown into a conversationalist. *Where did that come from? The new Jason can do anything.*

"Boy, you look like an engineer. You're probably making as much as me already. I'm so proud of you I could bust." Matt considered Jason's accomplishments almost as if they were his own.

"Thanks, Dad."

They sat down.

Matt couldn't resist falling into being a parent, maybe a bad parent, delving into old history.

"You know, there was a time when I wouldn't have guessed you would make it this far."

Jason looked annoyed. "You're not still mad about my freshman year, are you? That was six years ago. I took all those courses over."

"Never mind. I'm—I'm sorry, really. I shouldn't have brought that up." Matt could have kicked himself. He paused and wondered where to go from there.

"I hereby declare you are forgiven all adolescent misdemeanors. You're a man now. Independent. I misspoke." Matt smiled and waved his hand in a mock two-fingered blessing.

"Even the one when I shot out the Gilberts' basement window with my BB gun?"

It was a joke. Matt realized Jason was helping. "Even that one, you bad kid."

They laughed it off.

Home that night, when Janet, his wife, went to bed, their house seemed empty. Erin, their daughter, a senior at Michigan State, was at school. Matt listened to the soft venting of his computer fan in his den. An old mouse-harkened file appeared on his monitor. It was an unfinished work, an undeveloped concept that Matt had never shown to anyone.

"This was a total waste," he said to himself. "Fizzled out."

It was one of those mini advice books, planned as a four-by-six-inch thumb-through, entitled *A Father's Little Book of Advice for his Son's Freshman Year*. After a short introduction, the beginning aphorism was

> 1. Study first. Make time to study. Don't do it after something. Do it; then do something else. Make it number one. Get your stuff together and walk yourself over to your study area and sit your butt down. You must make yourself do this. It will get easier as you develop the habit.

Was it the conversation earlier today that had him

surfacing this file? Certainly, the season for advising his children about college was over. But despite the late hour, Matt couldn't resist going over the whole thing once again, one last time before deleting it, wiping it out as if it had never happened. The notion for his book came from workbooks and self-help books for college students and the small advice books on life in general. Little books of prudent wisdom, they are often bought as gifts. Matt conceived of his book when Jason had his troubles.

> 2. Get up and go to class. Drag yourself there. Absolutely commit yourself to getting to class. Go tired, go hungry, go hungover, go a little sick. Try not to cut any classes—zero. Save your cuts. Call a classmate when you do miss, or go see the professor. (Be careful about classmates; they may mislead you.)

Erin had done fine in college, and he had forgotten about his book. But bad starts for men seemed to run in his family. When did it start for him? Ah, it all fell apart, the shit hit the fan, in June 1966. He was a lifeguard at the city pool, and he waited for the bad news.

The blindingly bright city pool was a mass of kids jumping in, splashing, yelling, some even swimming. There were lines of five or six to get on the diving boards, two low and one high in center. The angled five o'clock glare of the sun made it impossible to see if one kid was jumping on another.

"Did you see Becky Garfield go off the high dive and lose the top of her bathing suit?" Jerry, his fellow lifeguard, said. Jerry came around, changing sides on the high guard chair on the deep end, meaning Matt was now off for the day. Both sunglassed young men were bronzed and glistening with a mixture of baby oil and iodine that was in vogue as sun lotion in the sixties. Matt's light brown hair was bleached in streaks by the sun.

"Nope. I saw her diving down to retrieve it, but I missed the best part. I saw her last time. She loses it at least twice a week and the guys watch her every time she goes up the ladder. Don't get too hot for that jailbait, now." Matt failed to laugh at his own joke, although Jerry chuckled.

Matt climbed down from his chair. He had worked the morning swimming lessons and guarded in the afternoon, and he was tired. He sat in the grass in front of the bathhouse, not wanting to go home right away. He calculated that the grade report, addressed to his parents, would arrive today, and he couldn't face going home. He sat and waited and wondered what would happen to his life. What would he do? He was at such lose ends that felt he could float away or shrink into oblivion, disappearing into the ground. He had lost his train of progress, lost his plan for life, lost his identity. He sat.

Maybe by some miracle he would just skim by. Looking up the pool's service drive, he saw his father's big Olds 98 turn in from the street. He knew what it meant—flunk out. Why did the grades have to come to his dad? Matt was nineteen. Why couldn't he at least get to open them first and learn his fate before anyone else. The grades were his, regardless of who paid the tuition. This was dishonoring. He felt like the lowest, dumbest person in the world.

In two days, his identity problems changed. He opened a letter that *was* addressed him that began "Your friends and neighbors have selected you …" A line from *King Lear* popped into his mind—one little thing he remembered from his poor studies: "The worst is not so long as we can say, 'It is the worst.'"

> 14. Self- or life loathing. This may not be your problem now, but everyone goes through it sometime. Try to stay positive. Studying will help. Exercise a little. Study, workout, eat some good food, get to bed early. Call someone if you need to. Tomorrow is another day.

It was Saturday, and Matt had met the mail truck at the box and brought the mail into kitchen. Jason was waiting.

"Give it to me, Dad. It's addressed to me."

"I wasn't going to open it." He almost had. As college funder, he felt entitled.

The first-semester grades came in an envelope of enfolding carbons addressed to Jason, the student, who after all was the legal adult to whom the grades belonged. Times had changed. After tearing the envelope apart, he read the contents and dropped it on the table without comment, more or less for others to read. When Matt saw the grades, his emotions grew distorted, like the sound that results when the volume is maximized on a miniature radio. He was astounded at the lowness of the grades; Jason failed two classes, received a D in one, and had a C in a fourth for an accumulated average much lower than Matt had ever received. *He even failed physical education. How do you do that?*

"What will you do, Jason?" Matt asked. "Will you go back? Can you go back? Maybe you should sit out for a while. Get a job and try the community college."

"I don't want to talk about it." Jason went to his room and shut the door.

Matt was profoundly sorry for his son, knowing what he might go through. Jason's whole life would be changed if he couldn't hack it at college. At the same time, Matt was angry with Jason for putting himself in such a position. But he was more worried than angry.

"Keep an eye on Jason," he said to Janet.

"Why? Is he going to do something? Seems like he already did it, or didn't do it."

"Bad news does funny things to young people. Just watch him."

Jason overheard some of this or sensed what the muffled conversation was about. He shook his head and told them, "You don't have to do that. I'm okay."

In fact he was okay, and this astounded Matt as well. Jason explained he could retake the courses and the new grades would replace the old grades as if he had never taken the first courses. His son simply shrugged it off.

Then Matt was mad about the money, but he forced himself to cool it and postpone the money discussion for a while. He would talk after he decided what he should say. Janet had let him know they were on the same page. Most of all, Matt feared permanently alienating his son. He refused to reprise the role of his own father. But once or twice, he thought of smacking Jason upside the head and clamping down on him in every way. Matt could still play the tough buck sergeant if he wanted. Should he should jerk Jason's ungrateful ass out of school and make him work for a living? Make him take out student loans and pay his own way?

Jason seemed to have no sense of the dishonor, let alone a sense of loss of time in life, worry about getting behind his peers, and all the money wasted. The family could afford it, but not without some sacrifice. On the whole, the larger effect was on Matt. It seemed to invalidate half his life. Jason, with everything going for him, failed the same way Matt had. Matt had worked with Jason from elementary school on to help him do well when he hit college. Jason should have succeeded.

If Matt could live part of his life over, he would go back to the first day of college. He could have done anything, been anything. But he didn't take advantage. He wasn't equipped. Couldn't get it done. He wouldn't change meeting his wife or having his family; he would still do that, but he would change the other stuff and be more successful.

29. Keep up with the assignments. Don't get behind. It will take more energy to catch up, and it won't be as good. In language and math classes it is critical to stay caught up, but it's important in every class. In middle age, I still have bad dreams about being behind in a college class.

34. Keep regular hours. Don't stay up too late. Nothing good happens after one in the morning. If you sleep in on weekends, it will throw your class days off. Sleeping can be a studying avoidance behavior. Recreational sleeping is no good. Stay up during the day; sleep at night.

"I blame Art and Dorothy." Janet, spitting bullets, charged Matt's parents out of the blue. She, like Matt, didn't want to take it out on Jason. "They screwed up your start at college, and somehow you passed it on to Jason. Osmosis or modeling or reverse psychology or something."

"He doesn't even know how bad I did."

"Yes he does. What is he supposed to think when you worked with him in high school? Went over his algebra with him so often, science fairs, special projects. And you went over that *How to Study in College* book with him last summer. He's doing just what you were telling him not to do."

"I don't think he's that complicated, and he doesn't have the Art and Dorothy kicker. Our marriage has been pretty good, and we stayed together. We've paid a lot of attention to him. Went to all his sports stuff and concerts. He has no bad habits. I drank like mad and just fucked off while A and D were oblivious."

"He's been fucking off too. I don't think he drinks much or smokes pot, but maybe he does. We wouldn't know."

"Oh, I think we'd know. I was dead in the water when I left high school. If I had had a shred of self-discipline, I might have worked it out. But Jason, he was ready. We got him ready."

"Apparently not. He seems to have inherited your self-discipline as an eighteen-year-old."

> 35. College life is a paradox. To paraphrase *A Tale of Two Cities*, it is the best of times and the worst of times. It can be the most fun you ever had and the most depressed you will ever be. Be prepared for ups and downs, and remember that both are temporary.

Later that evening, Matt's mind wandered from the winter outside back to the bright days of Vietnam. He was sitting outside his hooch, reading *For Whom the Bell Tolls* in the intense Southeast Asian heat after a downpour. He reflected that being in-country wasn't so bad. Reading a war novel in a war. Not that much to do right now. There had been just a few books left in the cardboard box that was passed around, but he got the one he would have picked anyway.

'Nam was like a Midwestern summer, only more humid, and the sun was right on top of the firebase. The mud and sand were drying up in the heat. Someone's big reel-to-reel tape stereo played the loud, churchy Hammond organ intro to "A Whiter Shade of Pale." You could hear the spinning-speaker effect across the compound.

Matt broke off the memory and went out to the garage to retrieve a glove he had left in the car.

> 39. Set a specific schedule to do your laundry. Do it every week. Take books and study. Plan for laundry. Sometimes you can meet people (sometimes cool girls) while doing your laundry.

> 40. Go to the library. Have a scheduled time for this. Go the library every night after dinner and stay till ten every night, except Friday and Saturday. Go during the day and one weekend day. Go more during test study periods and when you are writing papers. Or find an equally good place to study.

In the bedroom later, Janet asked, "Is anything wrong?" Speaking as she was, waiting to put on the top of her pajamas, the question had extra meaning.

"No, nothing's wrong," Matt was still dressed, not planning on going to bed for a while. "I'm just kind of worn out." He knew what she was getting at. She meant they had not been intimate for weeks. Matt just didn't feel like it. The urge didn't come to him, not that he didn't appreciate Janet, and not that good sex wouldn't have made him feel better. Once, he had started the preliminaries, but his heart wasn't in it. Not much response from Janet either. Hectic holidays, guests, and kids in the house.

Life continued much as normal through the holiday season and into the first week of the new year. Matt and Janet felt ill at ease with Jason, giving him significant gifts at Christmas while he seemed to take his situation very lightly. Matt and Janet didn't argue, but a certain dullness crept into whatever they did. Life's passions fell back to a lower mean. Certain topics couldn't be started since they led to arguments and pessimistic, fatalistic judgments. Life's decisions were pushed back. Grandmothers' questions were sidestepped. They had been told that Jason hadn't done very well, not that he had done *god-awful terrible*.

Jason spent most of his time in his room and then went out with his friends. He stayed out late but did not come home drunk or high. He slept late also. He watched TV in the basement rec room and fixed his own meals—except for dinner, which he ate with his family though he hardly said a thing at the table.

After Matt discussed the problem and its ramifications with Jason, what could they talk about? Not college, not the future, not money, not much of anything. All discussions seemed to lead back to the grades. Almost any conversation seemed patronizing or like harping at him.

Matt stayed up later at night, hoping to get a word with Jason, make some contact, sometimes with the television on or reading the newspapers or a book. Jason usually outlasted him, coming home well after midnight, keeping college hours. When Jason came home while Matt was still up, he said as little as possible and went down to the basement to play a Nintendo zip-zap game. Day after day, the Christmas break dragged on.

Matt considered that things could have been worse with Jason. He wasn't hurt, wasn't on drugs, wasn't in trouble with the law, wasn't suicidal. *Count your blessings.* Still, Matt's feelings were like a grief he couldn't master. Everyone was handling this better than he was.

Ennui worked into every aspect of Matt's life. He exercised less than normal, although he tried to at least walk every day. During the holidays, consistent exercise seemed impossible, but he wasn't getting fat. He didn't eat or drink so much, considering it was the holidays, a period when he habitually put on a few pounds. He forced himself to work on projects around the house, and he cleaned up both his work office and his home den, keeping busy.

> 45. You have too much stuff! If you just use everything occasionally—the TV, the videotapes, the CDs, all the computer software, the Internet, Nintendo, music programs, racquetball and tennis rackets, your own telephone, Rollerblades—you won't have time to study. You can beat this

> if you study first. Then, if there's time, you
> can use some of your stuff.

Jason's university didn't start again until the second week in January, and it took most of the day to drive there, unpack, and drive back. Janet decided to forgo the journey and stay home with Erin, whose school started the following week. A long winter drive on the interstate is never pleasant. Matt did just under eighty miles an hour most of the way. He tried to think of something to say that hadn't been said. Wisely, he said little; he talked about the traffic and the light snow that blew off and on. Most of the way, Jason wore earphones, listening to his music, blocking any communication.

Two men on a mission, they ate lunch at Wendy's mostly in silence. Jason drove the second leg. *Leaving the earphones off doesn't improve his conversation*, Matt thought. As an unspoken compromise, they kept the radio off.

When they reached the dorm, Matt helped Jason haul his stuff up to his room. Matt suggested moving the computer and its stand over to another wall and to put the reading chair by the door so the room was more balanced and people could get in and out. Jason passively agreed, with some annoyance. Matt tried to talk with him about the importance of doing better, but he could tell it was pointless. Then he noticed Jason didn't have a desk lamp. *Of all things, trying to study in college without a lamp on your desk.* He told Jason he would be right back and went back down to the car and drove over to Wal-Mart. He walked through the aisles in a daze. There it was, a brass banker's lamp with a green shade. It was one last damn thing. It wouldn't be Matt's fault if Jason flunked out and put his life in the dumps. It wouldn't be because he lacked resources or support from his family. Matt's mind filled with the doubtful, anxious pain of a young man as he drove back to the dorm. By the time he parked outside the building, his head was so clouded he could barely get out of the car.

Reflexively he checked the backseat and he saw a bunch of Jason's stuff that he would have taken back home. Matt raked it all up and checked the trunk and the rest of the car again, and with the lamp, he scaled the stairs to the third-floor dorm room. Jason met him at the door and took all the things.

"Well, I guess this is it." Matt said. "I checked the trunk, too."

Jason said, "I think you got all of it." There was an awkward silence as these two men worked out how they would part.

"Well, take it easy. Study hard," Matt said. Tears welled up in his eyes. His shoulders and chest shuddered, and he turned so his son wouldn't see. "I can't do it for you" was all he could get out before he stepped to go.

"I know you can't. You don't have to." Jason said.

Matt didn't look back, because he didn't want Jason to see his contorted face and tears. He nodded but waved his arm and moved to the stairs and went down. He got in the car and drove as calmly as he could, thinking he could be observed from the window, but he parked around the corner as soon as he could find a space. He sobbed for a minute, and the catharsis was over. Then he started the car and pulled out for the long drive home.

What will happen to Jason if he can't make it in college? He would have to come home, work in crummy jobs. Get a little better job and settle down in his hometown. Jason had potential. He was smart, good with people, and seemed to have everything going for him. Now he would have to make up for his mistakes and lost opportunities. Would he take every wrong turn, make bad decisions, and waste every chance?

It all welled up into Matt again—from his own life of letting himself and his dysfunctional family down, being drafted and serving in Vietnam, working at hard jobs, grubbing for money, and having a little chip on his shoulder, which never did him any good. Eventually, he saved some money and, using the GI Bill, graduated late. He started life at twenty-six instead of twenty-two. He was glad of one thing. At least Jason wouldn't have to go to war.

More than once, Matt fought back more tears over the long drive back home that evening. He told himself, *It's not the responsibility of parents to pave the road and smooth out every bump for their children.*

He arrived home exhausted. He and Janet discussed the trip and Jason's attitude. They agreed Jason didn't have much of a chance of succeeding. They decided he would have done just as badly at the community college. He just wasn't ready. Janet went to bed, but Matt, though tired, couldn't settle down, couldn't relax.

He didn't get to bed until after midnight, and he had a few drinks to make himself sleepy.

> 48. Getting an A. It will take extra work. You just can't do everything you're supposed to do and then expect an A. Go for perfection. Papers will have to cover every aspect, a fourth or fifth idea (or more), and be polished. No typos, no misspellings, no formatting errors. No sloppiness. Give yourself an extra day of studying for a test—after you already know everything. Practice problems until you can do them without errors creeping in, not just until you understand the problems. If the professor wants a ten-to-twelve-page paper, make it twelve. Unless it is very tight and excellent, a ten-page paper will seem like a lesser effort. But don't throw in material that is not relevant. Your paper represents you.

That night Matt had the unprepared-for-class dream. He had forgotten to go to the previous class and arrived as a test was being handed out. His entire college career depended on that test, but the dream awaked enough of his brain to tell him it was a dream. He wasn't in class. *Shake it off.*

Matt sat in the sun after a rain, reading Hemingway. The churchy Hammond organ began to play, speakers spinning for a hollow effect, "A Whiter Shade of Pale."

"*Incoming!*"

He didn't react in the first second. *What? It can't be. It's too nice out here, listening to music.* But he knew you could see mortar rounds on the way, even when you weren't quite sure whether you heard them fired out in the jungle. They make a high arch in the sky. *Boom!* More yells of *"Incoming!"* He ran from his hooch area as mortar rounds began bursting all over. *Boom! Boom!* Everyone was running for the bunkers and the trenches. *Boom!* A mortar round blasted up a ton of sand forty yards away as he dove into the trench. Staff Sergeant Cates was standing on top of a bunker, giving orders to get the hell underground and to get on the radio and call in an air strike. *Boom! Boom! Boom!* Getting closer!

Boom! Cates was blown off the bunker, landing right on top of Matt with about half the bunker dirt. Another round exploded almost on them. From the bottom of the trench, Matt, shocked from the blast and the continuing barrages, scrambled to keep from being buried alive and suffocated by the sergeant's body. *Boom!* The earth blown into the trench and the collapsing walls fell down on him. His nostrils, eyes, and mouth filled with dirt. He was drenched with water from the trench floor. No, not water. Something else.

To keep himself digging and churning to the surface, he yelled, "It's not my blood. It's not my blood. It's not my blood." He chanted this to convince himself he was alive, not buried, not blasted to pieces, and not bleeding buckets. He made it to the surface. *Boom! Boom!* Digging now to get back under the ground, soldiers screaming, the dirt became clods, the clods became shoes—digging under the dirt, the clothes, the shoes, the rods and racks, more screaming; digging down to Sergeant Cates' blasted face and huge, open, mangled, bloody body that flopped up at him. "It's not my blood! It's not my blood!"

And then Janet's voice. "You're okay! You're okay. Take it easy. Wake up, come back."

How can she be here? She'll get hurt! Boom! *Get down!*

Janet was yelling, "It's okay; you're here at home; you're home. You're dreaming; wake up, wake up."

She was down in the dirt of the hole with him with the shoes, the broken shoe racks, the pulled-down clothes. She was dragging him out, hauling him back. *What is she doing in Vietnam?* The explosions stopped; the winter night became silent, except for Matt's breathing.

He looked up from his closet floor to dark, snowy January in Michigan.

Janet turned on the light and pulled and guided him back to bed, and she held him as he twitched and shivered and returned to the here and now.

"You're okay. You're safe. You're home with me. I love you." She rubbed his head and neck and back, and he calmed more. They didn't speak for a few minutes, just rested and reset.

Matt raised his head. "I'm going downstairs for a drink of water."

"I'll come with you."

They sat in the living room with one lamp on. It was one thirty. He'd had this dream twice before. Once while still in Vietnam, once a couple of years after they were married, after he lost a job. In a little while, Matt was back to normal and they went back to bed.

After a few days Matt's libido returned. When summer grades arrived, Jason had done only slightly better than the first semester, but it didn't bother Matt. He decided Jason was in charge of his own life. Maybe it didn't make much difference today. Jason could graduate late; most people took more than four years. He wouldn't have to go to war. He could start at another college or go to community college or go to trade school, learn computers, and make more money that way.

Jason, after spending a summer at home working and realizing his friends were moving along, went back to school and made the big change. He retook most of his freshman courses and received Bs and some As. All the new grades wiped out his old courses, and his average was now over 3.0, but he was still a freshman. The family crisis lifted almost as quickly as it had fallen. Jason had fixed it himself, just as Matt had done thirty years before. The cost had just been family money, not years of fucking around and losing options. Jason took heavy loads, went to two summer sessions, and graduated in four and a half years. He did so well on the GRE that he was able to obtain a graduate assistantship at Michigan.

49. Plan projects ahead of time. Plan them soon after you receive the assignment. Use backward mapping. Plan out each step in

sequence from the project's end; use date deadlines. Start with the goal and work the steps for completion back to the present. Work it back and forth until you have a date for each step. This way, no matter the size of the task, you won't be overwhelmed.

Betraying Norman

DRIVING BACK FROM AN OUT-OF-TOWN MEETING, MY passenger and coworker told me something I didn't want to know. I admit I enjoyed knowing this seamy tidbit of his life, but my preference would have been to remain in ignorant bliss. I won't tell what he said. You can fill in your own sordid detail. Unless some forgotten nineteenth-century laws can be applied, it wasn't illegal. What struck me about the situation was that he had told me about it at all. If I divulged it, you might think less of him. Then again, these days, you may just think it's the way of the world.

When I asked him why he confided in me, he said that he knew I wouldn't tell anyone else. "You always keep confidences," he said. "You always have, and I wanted to talk about it."

We had worked together for many years, and while we were not close friends, we knew each other fairly well. He was right. I'm neither a gossip nor a moralist. His life is his own business. Besides, he will always be grateful to me for not telling and fear me a little because

I know. And telling just isn't good form. Why do I feel this way? One needs to examine one's basic motivations occasionally. Perhaps I've admired too many classy literary characters, or watched too many old movies, but I think my motivations are deeper-seated than that. Last night, relaxing and taking a break from reading in the hour before bed, I dug back into my psyche to trace my confidence-keeping origins. I tunneled clear back to my childhood and elementary school.

First grade was one of my best years. I had a nice teacher, Mrs. Bergman. Today, in my mind's eye, I can see that she was young and pretty. But to a six- or seven-year-old, she was an authoritative adult who was even older than my mother. She was not an imaginative teacher, but she worked hard to do a good job. I can remember her soft voice and genteel pronunciations. During my primary and secondary school years, I had teachers who were better and worse.

The pace in first grade was awfully slow not just for me but for my best friend too. He was John House, a big kid—big as a house, we thought. Early in first grade, he taught me to tie my shoes so I wouldn't have to wear loafers every day. I can remember my fumbling, skinny fingers getting it right for the first time—crossing the strings, pulling them tight, making a loop, pulling the other loop through, and pulling the knot tight.

Funny how things turn out. As mature men, John and I are roughly the same size. But in high school, he played football and I played clarinet. We were pals throughout the school years, but it has worked out that for decades, we have seen each other only at class reunions. Back in first grade, one experience we shared was being conferred a great honor and confidence by our classmate Norman.

Norman—I can't remember his last name—was perhaps the only boy in the class who was smaller than I. He was just a little thinner, a little shorter, very slight. Was his voice like mine, as high as the television antennas? No one knew. For more than two months, he had not said a word to anyone—not to Mrs. Bergman or to the kids. It was not for lack of coaxing that he didn't talk.

"What are you thinking, Norman? Please talk to me." Mrs. Bergman worked on him every day with her soft voice. "The other children would like to hear you talk. They want to be your friends, but they can't if you don't talk to them. No one will make fun of you, will we, class?

"We won't make fun of you, Norman," we all said.

She would talk with him privately and in the reading group. Once in a while, she would ask him a question in front of the whole class. The kids also tried to get him to talk.

"Why don't you say anything, Norman?" we asked. "We won't make fun of you," we said, individually reassuring him. Norman played dumb, not reacting at all, or he stared at the floor or the wall. Sometimes he shook his head. If pressured, he would put his head down on his crossed arms on his desk, and occasionally cry. A couple of times, Mrs. Bergman tried being stern with him, saying he would have to talk. She tried to get him to read jointly with another student or students. He just wouldn't cooperate.

It was apparent that Norman was of normal intelligence. He would get up and go to where he was supposed to go. He would nod or shake his head for answers. You could see in his eyes that he understood. There had been some progress. After a month, he would write in the workbooks, even do math, but he wouldn't talk. He put shyness off the gauge. We kids were unconcerned because we had our own things to learn. But from the beginning of school, Norman had not said a single word to anyone. I don't know how he had gotten into our class. Apparently, his mother had convinced the school that he could talk. Perhaps he talked at home. We kids didn't have the full story.

I can remember this short episode surprisingly well. On the playground at recess, Norman relaxed a little from his tense posture in class. At least he walked around sometimes. Usually, he spent most of his time swinging alone on the far side of the playground. But he was beginning to branch out, using the other equipment: the monkey bars, the teeter-totter, and the slide. He was mixing in a little, hanging around the outside of the activity, but still not speaking. More often than not, he was in my area. Perhaps he had an affinity for a fellow diminutive runt or hoped my gregariousness would rub off on him. Or maybe he just thought I was a nice kid. One day, Norman even joined our group at the witch's hat. It was the incident at the witch's hat that set in motion my betrayal of Norman.

Did you have a witch's hat on your playground? We made up the name. You don't see them anymore, and I know that this one was removed long ago. The legal climate doesn't allow them—like high-diving boards and those padded trampoline pits where you could rent bouncing time. The witch's hat was a hang-on merry-go-round. The double hand ring was suspended by chains and connected to a swivel atop a tall center pole. We would run around and swing up and down, pushing up and lifting our feet. If one side of the ring dipped, the other would raise, lifting the swinger. With a couple of other kids balanced around all sides, you could get it going pretty good. The overall silhouette was pointed, with the chains and hang rings making a short brim. We thought it looked like a witch's hat.

Basically, it was well designed, and no one was ever hurt using it correctly. It went round and round, up and down. It was fun. Did I mention that our school was brand-new? We were the first to use the classrooms and the first to run the witch's hat. Of course, in short order, when running around got old, we invented a more exciting use for this piece of equipment.

We got a big, strong kid, like my friend John House, to hook himself around the pole and pull one side of the ring into the pole. This would lift the far side up as high as seven or eight feet. Then we would get a light kid to hang on the end to be elevated and lift and swing him around until he was about to fly off. Other kids would help the big kid keep the rim pulled in and swing the ring around. Frequently, I was the light kid hanging on for dear life. I took some scary flights, and once I scraped up my face on a bad landing. But I knew how to get off when it went too high or too fast; you had to walk your hands down the ring toward the low end. If you yelled, they would let you down too, eventually.

Norman watched this go on for several days. Then, at everyone's urging and for reasons of his own, he allowed himself to be recruited as a light kid to ride the high end of the witch's hat. Perhaps he was following my example. I was taking a break from my last ride, and I watched the whole thing.

He grabbed on, and they got him up easily. John was around the pole, and five or six others helped him get it going. Up it went, higher than when I was on it because of there being less weight. Around and around it went, faster and faster. It made me dizzy just to watch. Centrifugal force was building up. The ring was swinging faster and higher than ever before. Norman didn't let go or say anything. By now, I would have bailed out. How long could this go on? He was stretched out straight. Then one hand came off! Norman was swinging around on one hand, but he wasn't yelling to be let down. As the witch's hat rotated, Norman was twisting and flopping around. *Soon his fingers will weaken and he'll go sailing off in the air,* I thought.

I yelled to John, "Let him down! Let go! He'll fly off and get hurt." John let go, and the ring came down just as Norman lost his grip and flew to a jarring landing. I figure he crunched his rear end pretty hard. Still he remained silent.

Tired of the witch's hat, we—John, Norman and myself—left it to the other kids. The three of us ended up together, climbing on the monkey bars. Norman seemed to be in a happy mood, and so was I.

"Hey, Norman, how did you like your launch?" I asked him.

I didn't expect an answer. But out of the clear blue, Norman said, "It was great."

Maybe he chose that moment to break his silence because we had just saved him from a twenty-foot flight and crash. It was a special moment after a big event. But the three of us had a sense that Norman's statement was said in confidence, away from all of the others. It was a moment of trust. John and I almost fell off the monkey bars.

"You can talk!"

Norman nodded. "Don't tell anybody."

"Okay. We won't tell," John said.

"Why don't you talk in class?" I asked.

Norman shook his head and looked down. "I just don't want to. I'll talk later."

John asked him more questions. Norman talked to John in quick birdlike spurts, with an occasional small stutter, but he could talk in complete sentences. It was something of a catharsis for him. It was fun for the three of us.

He had an accent that we little western Ohioans could recognize, even then, as slightly southern, and perhaps he was self-conscious of it. I remember being disappointed that his voice was in normal range—high, but lower than mine. As recess ended, he told us again not to tell anyone.

What happened next was not to my credit. It was out of good intentions that I felt I had to let the teacher know that Norman could talk, so he could talk to everyone. Also, I was proud that Norman had chosen John and me to speak to first. It was a special honor I wanted others to know about. I didn't wait for a good time to tell Mrs. Bergman, and I didn't pull her aside to inform her privately. I told her as soon as we came in.

"Mrs. Bergman, Norman can talk. He talked to both John and me on the monkey bars." I did this right in front of Norman and most of the class coming in from recess. John confirmed it. At this betrayal, pale Norman turned a whiter shade. He looked at me as if I had confirmed that the whole world could not be trusted.

The other kids heard of our breakthrough. A buzz crossed the room; Norman could talk. Norman could talk! The girls picked it up. "Oh, Norman can talk." Squeals led to a great crescendo of chatter.

Mrs. Bergman had to clap her hands. "Class, be quiet." To Norman, she said, "That's nice, Norman. Can you say something to me?" Everyone was watching. Norman looked away and didn't say a word. At this point, Mrs. Bergman lost it a little. "Please, Norman, you have to talk to me. I'm your teacher." Norman didn't respond. "Please talk to me. If you talk to your friends, then you can talk to me." Near tears herself, she continued to plead with him softly. "Come on, Norman. Talk to me."

Finally, she held him by the shoulders and said in a sterner voice, "Norman, you have to talk to me." Nothing from Norman. "I just don't know what to do. I guess you'll have to go see Mr. Hoffman." The threat of seeing the principal did not motivate Norman. His shyness was already at level ten. Mrs. Bergman tried several other times to get Norman to talk that day, but he wouldn't. Finally, Norman put his head down on his desk and kept it there. She didn't take him to Mr. Hoffman.

As far as I could attest, Norman never again spoke to anyone. A week later, after the two-day Thanksgiving holiday, he did not return to our class. I think he moved away, but Mrs. Bergman didn't tell us. She just stated that he wouldn't be coming back. I think his family was poor and transient, up from Kentucky.

Early experiences can leave permanent impressions, and I can say that Norman's silence and defeat at first grade has had a lasting effect on me. I felt I was to blame for Norman's continued reticence and disappearance from our class. Later Mrs. Bergman told John and me that we should have told her privately that Norman could talk. I know now the best thing would have been to keep it to myself. Norman eventually would have talked in class. He was warming up, and my revelation blew it. Then again, if I hadn't said anything, John would have. I just beat him to it, was all. It was a lesson for me though.

From that day, I've been careful with confidences. I can't say I never betrayed another, but when I did, it was either an accident or I was required to tell. I can remember Norman's whitened face and his look at his betrayer. But hell, that was first grade. John and I turned out okay. Norman probably did too.

Camille

THE FIRST TIME I MET CAMILLE, HER BOYFRIEND WAS asking that we three sleep together.

"Do you mind if Camille stays over in our bedroom tonight?" Big Teddy whispered politely, having met me at the door when he heard my Chevy chug in. He pulled me over to the kitchen area, which was open to the living room. "We've been sleeping, and she doesn't want to go back to her apartment across town. It's cold and rainy, too. I don't want to send her out."

My head was still in loud mode from bartending at the Canterbury Inn, and I had to focus on Big Teddy's quiet words. But the visiting little brother of George, another apartment mate, groaned and turned over on our living room couch.

"D'you work at the CI tonight? How come you're so late? We went to sleep."

Now Big Teddy was passing the blame to me for her still being here, as though, if I had returned earlier, as planned, this wouldn't be happening.

"She said it was okay if you sleep in your bed."

Nice of her. It was three o'clock on Friday—no, Saturday—morning, and I was dead tired from studying until ten at the library and then tending bar. I had gone down there late, hoping to be put to work if they were shorthanded. Even with the GI bill, Vietnam era, I had to scramble financially to stay in college. Student loans had yet to be invented.

Previously at lunch, Big Teddy asked me to vacate the bedroom until midnight on this November evening so he and Camille, his hot art major, could have a good time. I was still getting to know my three apartment sharers. They lived together last year, and as the FNG, I wanted to oblige and fit in. Two months ago, I answered an ad in the student newspaper, filling in the fourth spot when their guy changed his plans. Greenwood Apartments, Inc., a 180-unit complex, would charge the three of them for four beds, so they were happy to have me.

Big Teddy and I had two single beds in a large bedroom with a connected bath. I didn't mind him asking for the room. Eternally optimistic and ignoring the current state of my love life (absolute zero), I hoped he would reciprocate some night soon. My apartment-mates were seniors, twenty-one and twenty-two, while I was a junior, a little older, twenty-four, trying to make college life work for me the second time around.

Boy it was late, and I was going to pass out as soon as my head hit the pillow. *Who cares who's in the other bed or even what they are doing, for that matter.* But I was beginning to think that Big Teddy was the kind of guy who would take advantage if you let him. He was strong and broad-chested and presented an intimidating figure. I found this annoying, but I wanted to get along. He wasn't asking me to sleep out on the floor or the easy chair. It seemed kind of weird, but I told him okay. I walked through the bedroom to the bathroom in the dark, and I could just make out Camille covered up except for part of the side of her face.

"Hi, Camille." Might as well be sociable.

I heard a muffled "Hi" in return.

After traversing back to my bed, I went out like a light. And when I awoke, about eleven, I pulled on my jeans and stumbled out into the kitchen, yawning, rubbing my eyes, feeling deserted because the apartment was empty. All had flown, including George, his little brother, and Randy, our fourth. Disappointed that I had not met Camille, I whistled the melody from the Beatles' "Norwegian Wood" and went to brush my teeth.

Big Teddy and Camille had been dating for months, but I had never met her. They had used the bedroom, too, when they knew I was working, but she had always packed up before I got home. I had some late gigs: tending bar, writing up high school football games for the local paper as a stringer sportswriter, as well as feeding the dishwashing machine at Howard Johnson's. I was gone most of the time and usually studied at the library. With my blue-green portable Olivetti typewriter, I could write my papers and stories anywhere. It was like a laptop, only I had to erase my mistakes.

The following Monday afternoon, I found Camille drinking coffee at our kitchen table. "Hi, I'm Camille, the mysterious lady in the dark?" She said it as if it were a question, raising the pitch of her voice at the end of the sentence.

She wore a rust-colored, cowl-neck sweater with brown corduroy bell-bottom pants, a gold chain necklace, and little gold dot earrings. *Do you have to know art to look that good?*

"Oh, yeah, you're the woman I slept at the same time with."

She laughed.

"I'm Dennis." Big Teddy continued talking nonstop with Randy.

"So how was Vietnam?" She was interested in my history.

"Hot and muggy. Lots to keep you busy."

"It must have been exciting. Did you have to kill anybody?"

At this point, Big Teddy broke off with Randy and intervened, saying to her, "This is Dennis, my roomie." Then he turned to me and joked that he and Camille might need the bedroom that night. I looked again at Camille. She had long, fluffy red hair with lighter red streaks. Her skin was fair and smooth, and the gorgeous smile she flashed me took my breath away.

"Hey, you guys, I'm working till eleven at HoJo's,

so the chamber is yours. Try to clear out by then, okay?" It was the friendliest thing I could think to say.

Pale face flushing, Camille apologized for intruding last time, and sweeping back a lock of hair, she thanked me for not minding the inconvenience. "I'll get up and get out before you get home, next time. Don't worry."

"Not worried. It didn't give me nightmares." Trying to be clever. "Actually, I conked out right away and didn't even hear you guys get up." *Wow! I could go for this chick*. I hadn't been with a girl like that for a long time.

"That's good; we wouldn't want to keep you up." She gave me the ugly smile again, and I took a big breath.

Now frowning, Big Teddy seemed to disapprove of our brief interaction. Perhaps I was showing too much interest; eyes give you away. "Yeah, we wouldn't want to do that." Awkward silence.

"Well, nice meeting ya." I got up from the kitchen table and put on my coat. "Gotta go into town for something. See ya." I did have to put in my time sheet at the CI, but I wanted to get out of there. Cute girls flustered me. I was out of practice, and I didn't want to seem hot about my roommate's girl. *Wouldn't be her type anyway*.

Big Teddy and Camille fell in thick from the beginning of the semester, and I thought they would get engaged before he graduated in June. But, according to George, they had an emotional blowup over Thanksgiving with a yelling scene in University Union when classes resumed. The finale was at our place after the weekend. She came over, and they immediately sequestered in our bedroom. They started shouting. Randy turned up the TV loud so that he, George, and I could follow the *Monday Night Football* game. Camille came out, slamming the bedroom door behind her. She turned and yelled back at the door, "Fuck you, creep!"

We watched, moonfaced, TV blaring. Camille turned to leave but stopped after a few steps and faced back at us, straining for volume. "Fuck you guys too." Without further ceremony, she stormed out and slammed the door to our apartment as hard has she could.

Not easily rattled by anything, Big Teddy took his time inquiring after her, maybe a whole minute. "Did she leave?" He looked in the kitchen. We laughed out loud.

"You missed a very grand exit," Randy said. "If she busted that outside door, you're paying for it."

Big Teddy checked the door, shaking his head. Then, pacing back and forth across the living room, gesturing largely, he announced, "I'm not obligated to her! That's it. Good riddance to that that crazy bitch. I would never marry a goofball like her." He looked at me. "That's what she wants, you know. To get married, start a family. *Fuck no!*" Much relieved, he returned to our bedroom, closing the door hard. Fifteen minutes later, he rejoined us for ABC's Halftime Highlights, presented with commentary by Frank Gifford, Howard Cosell, and Dandy Don Meredith.

As close as Big Teddy and Camille seemed to be, I was surprised how cheerful he became without her in the two remaining weeks before Christmas break.

"Are you and Camille done now?" George, who liked to keep up-to-date on everyone, asked. He had come out of the kitchen area with his hand in a bag of potato chips.

Trying to study at the dining room table, I watched and listened with interest. White winter light was glaring over my shoulder into the apartment.

Big Teddy, standing in front of the TV, crossed his arms and turned toward the light. "Don't mention that broad's name to me."

"Okay, are you done with that red-headed chick?"

"Does a bear shit in the woods? Damn right." Big Teddy sat down on the couch and began watching TV.

Glad to be updated, I put my things together and went to the library.

For cold January, the month Nixon was sworn in, our apartment was girl-less. It was a busy month of starting new classes. Randy had a girlfriend back home, and George didn't date much. I had my hands full with my jobs and studies.

Big Teddy was busy, too, carrying a heavy load, trying to graduate in the spring. Also, he worked out and played indoor lacrosse so that he could stay on the lacrosse team in the spring. Not that he took athletics seriously; training rules were optional to him. He would always have a toke if someone offered, or a few beers on a day he wasn't playing.

On my twenty-fifth birthday, March 2, I got an assignment in my photojournalism class for a photo essay on an artistic work. The assignment was due in one week. I knew nothing about art, hadn't even thought about it. The closest I had come was a book about the art of the feature story—a book I bought, read, and took to heart. Mr. Massey, the photography instructor, was a squirrelly, balding, string-tied, cowboy-booted know-it-all with a big, curly-ended mustache. He wouldn't say what kind of art or where to photograph it. "This is a university, young journalists, go find." Desperate, but resourceful, I thought of Camille, who owed me one, and I called her up.

The voice that answered was elevated and weary, "Hello." Overcoming the impulse to hang up, I launched into my rehearsed spiel. "Hi, Camille, this is Dennis Mayor. You remember, Big Teddy's roommate?"

"Who is it again?"

"Dennis, the guy you slept at the same time with?" Lame, but it was the only reference I had with her.

"Okay, I remember." She laughed. "Are you still sleeping with strange women?"

"Every chance I get."

Laughter. "What do you want with me?"

"Well, the reason I'm calling is that I've got this photojournalism assignment. I'm supposed to photograph some sort of art. So I called you, the coolest artist I know. I want to photograph you in action, so to speak."

"Posing, you mean, for pictures?" She laughed again.

"Yeah, painting something."

She seemed to like the idea and told me she would be painting at the art building the following evening.

"That would be perfect," My heart beat faster, but I kept our discussion on an academic basis.

She set one condition. "Does your roommate know you are calling me?" She couldn't say his name.

"No, why should he? You guys broke up last year, didn't you?"

"Right," she said. "I don't want anything to do with him, okay?"

"No problem at all. We've roomed together since September, but we are not close friends. Not much in common."

"Good."

From the campus map, the big, new, glass-front art building turned out to be near the new administrative building. Camille's easel was on an aisle. She had a coveted slot near the north-facing window in a vast open studio, bigger than a basketball court, stretching out under florescent lights. There were rows and rows of easels and, in a back quarter, there were pottery wheels and kilns. She was painting a tall, wispy female figure looking at the stars in a long, flowing dress, various shades of blue.

"That's so, umm, arty," I said.

"What the hell do you know?"

"It's arty to me, and more importantly, it's sure to be arty to my sorry professor. You go ahead and dab around while I get started." I set up a ladder I found in the back and photographed her from above from all sides. Then I lay on the floor, shooting from below. As a joke, she swung her fringed bell-bottom pant leg over my head, straddling me for a second. I wasn't quick enough to snap that. Trying to look professional and artistic as I clicked off my photos, I asked her to address the canvas in different ways. Camille said lowly, "Anything you want," which I took to mean more than just posing for my photo essay.

"You like being photographed, don't you."

She nodded and turned to give me a profile, improving her posture and sticking out her chest. I was as interested in her figure as I was the art in progress, knowing Mr. Massey's mind-set. I had her stand back and sideways, studying her work, so that I could get both her and the painting. She and her canvas were tilted toward me a little less than forty-five degrees. It was one of these that I used as the primary shot in my essay for Mr. Massey.

After the machismo of army life, I found it hard to take orders from this scrawny, opinionated marionette. Grades for projects correlated with praising feminine pulchritude, and it was no use complaining about it. To get a good grade, I skinned the cat another way—with a photo of the type of person he liked. In his critique in front of the class, he admired my presentation of the image of Mickey Mouse on Camille's T-shirt. It jumped right out at him, he said. There appeared to be a paint spot on her shirt (which was actually a water spot on the negative, but he didn't catch it). All of this was black-and-white, taken with high-contrast journalism film, available at a discount in the photo lab.

I felt it was a good omen, my first A with Mr. Massey. Was Camille lucky for me? When I was a psychology major, my freshman choice, I would have called this noncontingent reinforcement. The A had nothing to do with her other than that my professor liked her boobs, which looked extra perky when shot from below. On the whole, I sensed that Camille wasn't a good-luck girl. But I had fallen for her before I left the art building—"Even so quickly may one catch the plague." We met for coffee the day after the photo shoot. The following Friday, we coffeed again after my morning class, before my afternoon shift at HoJo's. On Saturday I studied and did my laundry in the morning, worked at the CI in the afternoon, and took Camille to a party that night.

I picked her up in the student ghetto north of campus, at the vintage house she rented with four other girls. Their furniture was all secondhand stuff, contrasting with Greenwood's furnishing, which was all cheap modern. She showed me around on creaky floors. From a long closet crimped vertically by the slanted roof, she pulled out several of her paintings. My mind's eye recalls her best work as a cross between Klimt and Picasso in his blue period. All her figures were women, cool and aloof, floating or seeming to be about to float off, or in some relationship with the cosmos, this being the Age of Aquarius. I suppose she had specific assignments, like I did as a photographer, but she seemed to bring everything back to her reoccurring theme. I asked for a painting for my room, but she said she couldn't part with any, no doubt remembering who my roommate was.

"Won't your journalism photos be enough to remember me by?"

The statement seemed like a challenge.

Later we were back at her house in her room. I kissed her, and she kissed back. I started to unbutton her blouse. She seemed to like what I was doing, but she took my hand and said, "Not here. There's a house rule against sex and overnights. It's written into the lease."

"But everyone's gone." I kissed her again with urgency and feeling.

Letting go of my hand, she pulled me closer and whispered, "We have to be absolutely silent."

Slow and sensual comes along with soundlessness. Midway, someone came in the house and we shallow-breathed and slowed down. They left, and we resumed. It was wonderful.

There was never another opportunity in that house without tattletales around, so finding a place for lovemaking was problematic. Most of the time it was love by the dashboard lights. We parked my bench-seated, two-door '59 Impala, with a good heater, way out on the far side of lot 6, near the football stadium.

Backseat or front seat, she was flexible. When we were in funds, a couple of times, we got a room at the Red Shingle Inn, which used to be a chain Holiday Inn, then a Red Roof, cheaper and more run-down at each reincarnation. It was north of town, outside of the college district, at an interstate exit. I impressed her with my resourcefulness when I fixed the toilet chain with a paperclip after no one answered at the front desk. When Camille and I became intimate, she made a big deal of telling me that she was on birth control. "Thee this," she said thickly, pointing at the pill on her tongue one morning at the Red Shingle.

Of course, Camille and I couldn't come back to my room for fun, arranging for Big Teddy to vacate for the evening. She said everyone would think she was slutty, returning to shack up in the same room. I asked if she still had feelings for Big Teddy.

"He's a closed subject," she said. "And I don't want you talking to him about me, okay?" Despite her coolness about her old flame, there was still something in the background. Later, I came to think the feeling was probably more like hatred than anything else.

That night, we danced at the CI. When the band took a break after Blood, Sweat & Tears' "You've Made Me So Very Happy," we returned to our table and beers, and she brought up the photography again. "I didn't know you were going to show Big Teddy your journalism photos." She had a girlfriend who sat in the union at lunch with a gabby gang that included Big Teddy.

"I didn't show them to him on purpose. I was laying out my photo essay on the kitchen table, and he came over and checked them out. If it means anything to you, he seemed intrigued to see you as an artist, painting. He leaned over close and examined each one and asked what colors things were. He said it looked pretty good. Did he call you or something?"

"No, he didn't." She bristled at the idea. "I wouldn't talk to him, anyway. I don't care what he thinks." She refilled her glass with beer from our pitcher and gulped some down. Then she moved on to her favorite topic of conversation, the war in Vietnam.

Camille's politics were out there, left of McGovern somewhere, and she often ragged on my lingering support for the war. By that time it seemed everyone who mattered was weary of the conflict, realizing it was unwinnable and that the government had lied, murdered, bombed, and spayed toxic chemicals in our name. She complained about my decision not to go with her to SDS (Students for a Democratic Society) meetings.

"We should take over the administration building here, like at Harvard," she said. I reminded her that everyone had been arrested there and that a bunch of the SDS students had been hurt. She had no patience for the journalistic objectivism I maintained.

"Let's talk about something else," I suggested.

After another glass of beer, she smiled at me, took my hand, and asked, "Do you want to take some more photos?"

Okay, this is cool. "Yeah, why not? What should we shoot?"

"Let's have some excitement. Do something more artful. Would you like to do some figure photography of me in my bikini?" She straightened up, threw her shoulders back, and gestured toward me palms up.

Putting hand to chin, I nodded. "Okay, but it's too cold for the beach. How about lingerie at the Red Shingle. It's a good place." She agreed, and just like that we set it up. I didn't have to talk her into it. We discussed what we would need to take good photos.

This is going to be a gas. At the time, I was willing to play the photo artist, impressing her if I could. But in reality, photography was never going to be my main hustle; I was a writer. All I wanted to be was a good newspaper journalist, maybe write a novel or a journalistic book later. That was the extent of my occupational planning. For the business at hand, I prepared in advance by looking over two books in the library—*Photographing Women* and *Figure Photography*. So I came into the enterprise with some knowledge. I shot from every angle, which isn't far from art, using grainy black-and-white film. Camille advised me in my artistry, and we did our best to make a cheap motel room a studio. We borrowed some lights, two big Grecian urns, and a textured background from the art building, and I set them up and photographed her in black bra and bikini panties. It seemed so cool to me that she wore Lily of France, which I later learned you could buy at J. C. Penney. Many of the photos were taken at extreme angles, like those from over the ankle up to her face. Her body was tight from yoga, lithe, and thin, with some curves, but she was not muscular or athletic. I noticed she had firmed up for the photos, especially her abs and triceps.

We giggled and horsed around, and soon it morphed into no-clothes photos. We tried some humorous poses, which were mostly her idea: lying on bed sideways, facing away, one leg bent, shot level from the side with a fruited, dark, sangria-looking drink (Coke) sitting on her hip. From behind, I shot her with one foot in the shower, one buttock and most of upper body covered by shower curtain as she entered. We did some of her breasts as mountains and butt cheeks as valentine hearts. One had a very short focus on the tines of a fork on the side of a plate with bare boobs leaning over the plate, a little out of focus. Altogether arty.

"It's very liberating, posing in your birthday suit," she said.

I couldn't get naked photos developed anywhere I knew, and it was costly to do big prints. I slipped into the journalism photo lab late one night and developed the film and printed contact sheets from the negatives, producing many rows of photos not much larger than postage stamps. I had shot two rolls of thirty-six exposures, which seemed like a lot, but a true photo shoot might take hundreds. To look at them closely, we needed a magnifying glass, so we talked over them like Natasha and Boris. We discussed selling them to photography magazines, but I never sent them out. I was a journalist, not a photographer or a pornographer. We were just having some fun.

Camille's aspirations for life weren't very different from mine. I wanted to be a journalist; she, an artist. Neither of us was interested in teaching. She seemed pretty crazy for an American girl, and I loved her for it. After Vietnam, sweet virgins were in no way appealing—repugnant, actually. Camille had some interests I didn't share. Once she suggested we smoke a joint. She had the goods and was bummed when I declined. So she came down, so to speak, to my level, missing the other lifestyle all the while. I wasn't good with cannabis. I always seemed to get a hangover, exacerbated from the booze I drank with it. Then I seemed to be naturally stoned for a couple of days, a little slow on everything.

After thinking that Big Teddy was no longer interested in Camille, it irked me when he found out about our more recent photo shoot and wanted to see the results.

"Do you have some more photos of Camille?" he asked me when we met in the parking lot outside our apartment. He might have been waiting in ambush.

"No. What are you talking about?" I didn't feel obligated to tell Big Teddy the truth, and I didn't like being confronted like this. Obviously, Camille had told someone about the photos and it had gotten back to him.

"Come on. I know you took some good ones. Let me see them."

"How do you know that?"

"A little bird told me. What's the difference? I know you took some good ones. How good are they?"

"The birdie was putting you on. She must have had a good laugh. I didn't take any more." He hadn't moved, and we were still at my car.

"Look, open your trunk and show me what you got. I know they're in there."

How did he know where they were? Did he search my stuff? Only Camille knew I kept them there.

"Nope. There are no more photos; forget it." I started to go into the apartment.

"Come on." He moved to block me.

"No. Do you mind?" I moved farther around him, and he moved off. No way on earth I was showing him anything.

Later, he apologized and said he was jealous when he heard I was dating Camille, but then got over it. "I'm glad you two are going out," he said. I accepted his apology. He wasn't very deep, and emotional subtleties just went over his head. He was a business major, not a ponderer of life's complexities. All he wanted to do in life was go back to his hometown and fit into the business community. We didn't keep in contact over the years, but I saw him once more after he graduated.

Camille admitted to mentioning the photo session to her girlfriend, but said she swore her to secrecy.

Camille and I both became busier after that. We both had large semester-end papers, projects, and finals, plus I had stories to write, photographs to refine, and work to do. Late one Friday afternoon, I played in a pickup basketball game in the men's gym; I was invited to stop in that night at a fraternity party at the next complex over from Greenwood, the Wellington Apartments, which were brand-new, plusher, and higher in rent. Camille said she had to study, and she didn't like that I was going to the party without her. "I'm just going to stop in and say hi to some friends," I told her. I got there fairly late, near eleven, and the party was cool. They had a keg. I knew several of the frat brothers through playing basketball.

No one ever seems to mind when uninvited girls show up at a party, and here was Camille with a girlfriend. She said she was just dropping by to see if there were any cute guys. A little later, she decided to kiss one of the fraternity brothers, and they began making out. I assumed she was high. It was hard to tell with her. When she came up for air, I offered to take her home. "No. I'm not with you," she said, and she turned back to talk with the frat boy, who most partygoers—but apparently not Camille—knew was gay, or perhaps bi. I left and went down to the CI, seeking work, but I wasn't needed there either.

The next day, about noon, she called me and said she wanted all the pictures and the negatives I took of her. I had about had it with Camille and her smooching of fraternity boys. "Does this mean we're finished?" I tried to sound ironic, although I still wanted to stay together, if we could.

In a sad voice, she said she left the party soon after I

did and went to my apartment. "Your car wasn't there. I wanted to say I was sorry." Long pause. "Can we go out? We can talk and you can give me the photos."

"All right," I acted as if I were giving in. "Let's. I'll pick you up. You know I would never embarrass you with the photos."

She sighed. "I know you wouldn't, but I'm getting paranoid about them, and I want to burn them up."

Okay, she can have them. I put the contact sheets with the negatives in a big envelope and gave them to her when she got in the car.

"Thank you." She kissed me. "Why don't we do something."

It was drizzling, and there was nothing to do but go to the campus movie, which turned out to be a real stinker: Andy Warhol's trashy *Flesh*. After about thirty minutes we looked at each other and shook our heads. She held her hand up as a microphone, announcing, "And the winner for the worst film ever is ..." She motioned to me, handing over the microphone.

"*Flesh*. Thank you, Andy, come up and take a bow." I put the mike in my armpit, and we both clapped. Some other people got up to leave as we did.

Except for this exchange, our doomed relationship might have been resurrected better if we'd stared at a hundred Campbell's soup cans for half an hour. We went to a college bar, not the CI, and split our usual small pitcher of watery draft. Later, we parked my Chevy in the back of lot 6, once again making love by the dashboard lights, turning on the heater briefly to take out the night's dampness. The sex was sweet and athletic, and it didn't seem like a good-bye fuck. Maybe we went out this time just because we had nothing else to do and neither of us wanted to be alone.

Finals were over; it was mid-June, and the semester was ending. Camille needed just a few courses to graduate in December, whereas I needed two semesters, plus three courses that summer. She went home, where she had a job, and gave me her family telephone number. "Don't call me. It gets complicated with my parents. I'll call you." She said would come back to campus periodically. I remained at the university, taking summer courses, running the dishwashing machine, and bartending.

She did call me once a week, and we talked, but she could never arrange to get back to campus. By the end of July, I longed to see her in the flesh. Also, I wanted to meet her family and see her place. I knew almost nothing about her home life.

"I love you. Don't you miss me? We need to see each other to keep our relationship going." I didn't like whining and begging, but it was that or nothing. "If you're not coming up to campus, I'm coming down to you. Tomorrow."

"All right. I do miss you, but I can't borrow the car for a whole day and night right now."

She said to come down after dinner on Saturday, and we could go out for a movie or something, not staying out late. She said her parents went to church on Sunday and she didn't want to sleep in.

When I arrived, she scurried down the front porch steps to meet me, her long red hair flowing, wearing a lime-green tank top and blue jeans. An older man came to the door and watched her kiss me.

"That's my dad; you can meet him later. Let's go."

We got in the car right away and drove off. She said her parents were mad at her because her mother had found her asleep on the couch that morning. We drove around for a long time, talking about the campus in the summer, my jobs, and her summer job in a department store. I wanted to make love, but she didn't. When I brought her home about midnight, she whisked me into the kitchen and we talked in lowered voices, not wanting to wake her parents. The air conditioning was set too cold, and she went to get a sweater, returning in her pajamas and a robe. Apparently, she didn't want me to stay very long. After a few minutes, I kissed her good-bye and turned to go. "I'll let myself out."

"I'll call you." She motioned with her hand up to her ear.

Yeah right, like before. What good will that do? I was suddenly miserable and angry, as well as horny. She didn't follow me to the door. I stepped outside and, closing the door tight, peeked back in, hoping to get one last glimpse of her.

Sighing in frustration, I took a big breath as the ninety-degree heat and heavy humidity enveloped me. Then the red-haired, graying, balding, overweight, middle-aged man I had seen earlier from the car greeted me from the side of the porch. He took off his reading glasses and put down a *Sports Illustrated* magazine.

"Can't you leave her alone?" He arose from the chair where he had been sitting, illumined by the single porch light.

"Excuse me?" I said, not following.

"Her mother flew her down to a hospital in Puerto Rico for you. Ended it all, and you got off with no responsibility. What else do you want? Do you know what you did to her?"

"What are you talking about?"

"Do you know what you did to our family? We're Catholic, or were Catholic. I don't know what we are now. And it's all because of you. Why did you come here? Haven't you done enough damage? You don't love Camille. We thought you were done with her. You can't start up with her again, now. Why don't you just leave and never bother her again?"

"What? Are you crazy?"

He stepped forward. "You know, your baby," he said, trying to sound confident with his voice fluttering.

"Not *my* baby."

"You son of a bitch!" He cranked back and swung a big roundhouse right at me. It was surreal. How odd it was that he expected me to wait for his fist to hit my face. I pulled my head back like Muhammad Ali, the punch whizzing by. As I stepped to the side, his weight and force followed his fist, and I pushed him in the direction he was going. His head knocked hard against the circular porch post, and he fell to the floor, shaking the whole house. When he righted himself, pulling up on the railing, he had a red scrape above his left eye. (It turned Technicolor later, according to Camille.) Focusing again, he started sizing me up, closing the distance.

I shoved him back into a porch chair. "Sit down, old man, and stay there." I trotted down the porch stairs and called over my shoulder, "Like I said, you got the wrong guy, dumbass." I walked quick time to my car and drove off sharply, thinking he might want to continue in the yard. Oddly, I felt bad calling my girlfriend's father a dumbass, but the motherfucker had it coming. I had already graced his ass by not fucking him up.

"Bastard! Don't come back," he had yelled from the porch steps, shaking his fist.

Well! He certainly showed me. But he might have at least introduced himself. I figured the abortion was Big Teddy's, remembering the post-Thanksgiving fight and breakup. It wasn't my creation if Camille was truthful about the birth control. She never gave me a reason to think I caused the pregnancy.

I phoned her the next morning, and her mother answered on the first ring. She said Camille was out, so I asked that Camille call me. No call all day and night. I tried again the following day, and Camille answered and claimed she hadn't gotten the message.

"I can't talk very long now," she said, sounding exasperated that she had to deal with me at all.

I asked her about the abortion.

"That's none of your business—don't ask me about that. I didn't have an abortion, and don't tell anyone I did." Angry now, she said that her parents had almost filed an assault charge on me. "Did you have to hit my dad?"

I told her what happened and asked her to check the post where he went down—"there's probably a mark"—and to please try to straighten things out. She acted as though she wasn't sure what to believe, but she knew the truth. She said she had to go and that she would call me the next day.

When she didn't call, I felt like an empty, overturned trash can rolled out in the street. I began to think, *Was it my kid? Shouldn't I have been consulted?* If she could convince me that she loved me, I'd marry her. Then I reviewed the facts again. *It couldn't be mine, and what could I do now, anyway.*

Over the next two days, I called her six times. The phone just rang and rang. It seems primitive that there were no answering machines then. Her rejection was complete. It hurt me down to my toes. But after the porch incident, what did I expect? For a while, I thought of driving down and confronting her—but for what purpose? I knew all the answers. There were extra hours available at HoJo's, and I made myself busy enough that I couldn't think about her all the time. Then nature provided a sign when Hurricane Camille devastated the Mississippi delta. *Yes, good riddance* was my final, sad conclusion, although I felt worse about it than Big Teddy sounded when he said it. I stopped calling her and tore up the letter I had composed.

By fall, I was seeing a girl who used me better. I don't know if Camille returned to school. Once in a while, driving along, I noticed the art building and thought of her. I hope she went to New York, got an artistic job, and sold her paintings, although I doubt it. More likely, she continued to work in that hometown store and married some insurance peddler—someone who shared her recreational interests and appreciated the avant-garde in her.

The following June, in the month I graduated and took up a reporter's job, I was invited to Big Teddy's wedding to his high school sweetheart (to whom he had been attached all the time he was balling Camille). The huge ceremony was in a little town halfway across the state. Looking disappointed when he first saw me— maybe he thought I would bring Camille—Big Teddy perked up and said hello to my new steady girlfriend. Later, when he had a chance, he asked privately, "What about you and Camille? D'you ever see her?"

Not giving anything away, I told him I had lost track of her.

"I didn't ask, okay," he said with a wink.

"Okay, Big Teddy." I winked back.

Manhattan Mendicant

"THERE'S THAT BUM, RIGHT WHERE HE ALWAYS IS." DAN pointed out the panhandler to Karen, his wife, as they walked past the beggar's corner situation in lower Manhattan. He had noticed him twice before on business trips to the city.

"Don't call him that," Karen said. "He might hear you. Nobody should be a bum. If you have to call him anything, call him a mendicant." She paused, as they had to make way for a woman in a big coat carrying two shopping bags and a big purse. "This is New York; you can upgrade him."

Dan smiled and chuckled, not buying it. *A bum is a bum. Why doesn't he get a job? It would be just the same, hanging out in the same place every day, doing your duty, putting in your time.* It was overcast and freezing cold. Clouds of steam lifted through the manhole covers as masses of people hurried by, all dressed in the city's black uniform. The wretch, also in black, kept at it, standing with no breaks, as far as Dan could tell. He estimated that the man was about his own age and size.

There but for the grace of God go I …. No, he corrected himself. *I could never be like that.*

As Dan and Karen approached the man's corner eddy, against the wall of a tall office building dwarfed by the Twin Towers it faced, they could hear his whining, nasal voice. They stayed a dozen feet out to the street curb, keeping their distance. "I need something to *eeeat*," the man said. "You got any spare change?" He waited a beat, then, "I just need a couple of dollars to get something to *eeeat*." He didn't vary his chant or mantra. By the time he parroted these three sentences, the crowd flow brought new ears for his spiel. For those who slowed, each utterance wore on the ear, and it seemed more and more pathetic.

The man was there again in the afternoon. Dan and Karen were walkers, and shopping and lunch had brought them by this downtown block again. In midday, it was brighter, still cold and cloudy, but otherwise the situation was the same. This time the crowd traffic put them right up next to him.

"I need something to *eeeat*." It was louder and more annoying close-up. He displayed a look of exasperation for the passersby who didn't contribute.

"You got any spare change?" He took a breath and seemed to be trying to remember the third sentence. Then it came. "I just need a couple of dollars to get something to *eeeat*." The man had turned up the collar of his coat against the cold and perhaps for effect. His ears were pink, his nose was a little red, and he wore no hat. But he had longish, bushy hair, so perhaps his head was not so cold. He was decked out in a thick topcoat and a dark crew-neck sweater with no visible shirt. He wore no gloves, but he kept one hand in his coat pocket. He set a grubby coffee can at his feet for donations—maybe this was in case donators didn't want to touch his palm. Whenever there was a break in the people stream, he emptied the can into a bag he kept behind him; it never looked like he had too much.

Karen urged Dan onward. They had places to go and things to see—too few expensive New York minutes to waste considering a well-fed beggar on a street corner.

That night in bed at the hotel, waiting for sleep, after a long day and a big evening, Dan thought about the scrounger again. He had now seen the man over the Christmas season, in the rainy fall, and in the heat of the summer. The man kept at it but vacated the corner in the evening. Dan and Karen had taken a taxi down a parallel street, and Dan had looked down the cross street and saw that the beggar was absent. *No overtime for this character, although there's money to be made.* In this city, there were still lots of people around. *Does he have a territory? Could he get someone to fill in for him if he took time off? If I gave him some green stuff, could he be induced to take a break and explain his life situation? Maybe he wouldn't tell the truth or even know the truth. After all he's just a beggar on a street corner. Perhaps he is just another brain-addled druggie.*

Dan loved New York and resented that this mooch could live here when he, Dan, couldn't. It was back to the provinces in two days for Dan. Home was a small town in Michigan, an hour north of Detroit, near Lake Huron's shore. Dan couldn't afford to live in New York, as much as he would have liked to, and he could not change from his settled life now. Just a year after he started with his present agency, he'd had a job interview in New York, high up in one of the Twin Towers. He almost grabbed the ring, rang the bell, but the job was offered to someone else. It was one of the major disappointments of his life. Since then, he and Karen and their children had grown strong roots, and both he and Karen had vested in growing pension plans. Still Dan both envied and resented the mendicant's lot, and overall he found him repulsive. To be truthful, that asshole really got to him, and he could just spit. He didn't tell Karen how he felt. It was something he kept to himself, a hidden little dark spot on his persona.

If they didn't spend too much on other things, they could afford to visit New York, if they could find the time—kids like to go Disney World. *The mendicant lives his whole life in this exciting metropolis. All he has to do is stand on the corner and whine. Generous pedestrians put a lot in his can today. Perhaps on Saturday nights, he goes out for dinner and a Broadway show. Maybe he writes when he's away from his corner. Panhandling is just a sideline, something to keep food on the table while he creates the great American best seller. Does he have a family? Does he purchase health insurance? What is his profession on his tax return? "Mendicant"? Does he pay taxes? Someone should drop a dime on this guy with the IRS. He's really raking it in.*

Dan continued to wonder. *What is the overhead for*

this location? Does he intimidate other beggars? Pay police? Pay for protection? Or is that passé? What kind of person is he? Where is his self-respect? What is his contribution? He just annoys us. He's not even much of an example to use to rise above so that we thank our lucky stars we aren't in his situation. He's embarrassing to everyone. It's embarrassing that prosperous America still has beggars.

It's disgusting. They guy doesn't need to be out here. There are programs, like Social Security, that support disabled persons. He's just out here for extras, or he's out for drug money. He should get a job, be placed in supported employment. Pull his own weight, if he can. Get out of sight and stop bothering people.

They used the hop–on–hop–off bus a second time the next day, and its circuit brought them down to the World Trade Center. Rick saw the beggar was at his station, and he decided to get off, bringing Karen, to make a contribution. In their drive to New York, Dan and Karen had traveled from Michigan, through Ontario, and above Lake Erie, and had crossed at Niagara Falls. Dan took a *loonie*—a Canadian one-dollar brass coin with the queen on one side and a loon on the other—from his jacket pocket and chucked it into the beggar's can. It made a brassy clink. *Let the sponge figure it out.* Dan, the last of the big spenders, knew its current worth was sixty-three cents.

The mendicant looked down at the coin in his can and then at him.

"Fastidiousness by mendicants is prohibited," Dan

said. The beggar scrunched up his nose, waited a beat or two, and turned his head forward and began his chant again.

Karen gave Dan a little tug on the arm. "Very funny. Don't be mean," she said. "Do you think he'll get that? Come on."

Bringing a car into New York City had been a mistake, but Karen didn't like to fly. Using the car at all was a big hassle, parking was almost nonexistent, and storing it was expensive. After a late lunch the following day, they retrieved their car from an underground garage and drove for four hours before they stopped in upstate New York. Karen looked at Dan and then poked him in his side. "I need something to *eeeat*," she whined nasally. "You got any spare change?" she asked, wrinkling up her nose. It took Dan by surprise.

"Okay, let's quit that," he said. "Now he's got *us* talking that way." But it remained a little joke with them for a few weeks. Whenever either was hungry, one of them might say, "I just need a couple of dollars to get something to *eeeat*." It got old quickly, and Dan knew it wasn't nice.

On the morning of September 11, 2001, Dan was stuck in a staff meeting that had run long. The head of one of the working divisions returned from a personal break (during which she had sneaked out for half a cigarette) to say, "It just came over the radio." She was a little breathless. "Terrorists crashed an airliner into the World Trade Center." Dan thought immediately of the beggar, although the enormity of the disaster was still unfolding. From back home in small-town Michigan, comfortable, semisuccessful Dan hoped Cheap Charlie had hauled his ass away from the building before everything crashed down on him.

When the buildings fell, Dan took it almost as a personal calamity. *What were the last minutes like, caught in the upper floors, wondering if you would be saved, calling your wife on your cell phone, and the building collapsing? And those who jumped to their deaths before that? How bad, how fiery, and how hot must it have been to make jumping the better alternative?* Dan pictured the dependable mendicant, a whining island in a river of black-clothed Manhattanites, near ground zero. Dan imagined him looking up at the first plane crashing into the skyscraper as people scattered. *Did he run to get out of the way of the falling debris? Did he stick around until the first tower collapsed? Did he get far enough away? Was he enveloped and suffocated by the clouds of pulverized concrete? What happened to him?*

During the incessant TV rerunning of the planes crashing into the towers and the towers' ultimate breakdowns, Dan always looked for the mendicant's corner but could never quite figure it out. Videos were shot from odd angles, mostly focused far above street level, or they showed people running from the dust clouds without evident landmarks in view. Dan's heart sank every time he watched.

Dan and Karen did not return to New York until

the fall of the following year. Oddly, Karen found the courage to fly this time, cutting against the national trend for skittish fliers. Anxious to see how the city had recovered, they took the Gray Line double-decker, hop-on-hop-off bus downtown. From Times Square, they passed the Empire State Building (now the tallest in the city), and Madison Square Garden and the Flatiron Building, then the East Village, and down to Lower Manhattan. Finally, in the Financial District, Dan took a deep breath of relief when he spotted the man at a busy corner between Wall Street and Bowling Green Station. The guy seemed a little thinner, but otherwise no worse for wear. Dan smiled and choked up a little at this demonstrated resilience of mankind still bleating out, "I need something to *eeeat.* Got any spare change? I just need a couple of dollars to get something to *eeeat.*"

Dan got off, bringing the reluctant Karen. He watched the mendicant for a few seconds. Then he crowded in close and dropped a Ben Franklin in the guy's can. The mendicant blinked at the bill, raised his eyes to Dan, and said, "Th-th-thanks." A flicker of recognition ran across his face. As Dan turned to go, the man touched him on the shoulder, looked him in the eye again, and said quietly, almost confidentially, in his nasal voice, "Ff-fastidious b-b-beggars can't be ch-choosers, can they?"

Dan twisted back toward him, but the crowd pushed him and Karen along. The panhandler pocketed the bill and started his chant again. "I need something to *eeeat*" rang out with gusto. "Got any spare change? I just need a couple of dollars to get something to *eeeat*."

Karen took Dan's arm and pulled to get him to move on. Dan resisted at first, trying to work back to the beggar. Then he turned and went along. His shoulders relaxed, and he felt better.

Scarlet Amber

AT THE END OF A WOODED TRACK DOWN BY THE Olentangy north of town, the old-style white Beetle rocked gently in rhythm with Diana's breasts. Light summer breezed in through the window, and a redwing sang from the cattails. I slouched down in the middle of the backseat, and she sat astride; we had found the best way in cramped quarters. It was an afternoon delight by the deserted riverbank after our Wednesday-morning classes. The memory runs, again and again, in a continuous loop.

I should think about something else tonight at the beginning of the new millennium. That was 1970—so long ago it just isn't funny.

"You have the tickets?" Beth, my wife, asked half an hour ago as she quickly pulled her pajama top down over her head. She was sitting on her side of the bed, facing her dresser. As I stood in the doorway, there was a strong, messy odor of night cream or whatever she put on before bed.

"No, they are e–tickets. We pick them up at the airport." (You couldn't print them then.) She was letting me know this was my trip and that she was going reluctantly, so I reminded her, "You know, we agreed to go right after this case was settled. If you didn't want to go, you should have said so."

"Of course I want to go, but it just disrupts my whole life. I had the museum friends meeting, I had to get a sub for bridge, and I had to reschedule the carpet cleaning. Then I had drop out of the hospital tennis house party, and I had other plans, too." She paused and touched her alarm clock to see that it was set.

"Did you rent the car?" she said, returning to trip preparation. "We'll want to have a car down there." She was still facing the other way, working on a fingernail.

"We'll rent the car when we get down there, if we need it. There aren't many places to drive, anyway. We can take a cab." I stopped before I reminded her that we were going to Belize to hang out on the beach and scuba dive, not to auto-tour. Our resort was all–inclusive.

"I think we'll need a car anyway." Her head turned a little my way. "I feel so limited and confined if we don't have a car."

"Okay, as soon as we get down there, I'll rent one." She talked about one vacation when we didn't rent a car and we hardly saw anything but the hotel's beach and café.

"The banks are closed on Sunday, so you'll have to get the traveler's checks early Monday."

"I got them already. Everything is set." I said

goodnight and went downstairs. *After nearly thirty years of marriage, she thinks I don't know what she's doing. Or she doesn't care if I know, as long as I go back downstairs and let her read her book.*

As I was walking down the hall, she reminded me, "Don't forget to tell Heather that Rob called."

Heather is our daughter, home for the weekend, out late with friends, keeping college hours. I hope to stay up and see her, say goodnight, but I'm tired. I miss her when she is away at college, and talking with her at dinner reminded me how much. Although she came home this weekend, her relationship with Rob, her high school beau, is on the rocks. She's a freshman at State. He works full-time and goes to the community college. She could do worse than the loving, earnest Rob, but I know parents are never good evaluators of children's love lives—of what floats their boats, melts their gruyère.

Gazing through the bay window of my den, past the snowy gazebo and trees in our backyard and the yards of my neighbors down the hill, I sit in my recliner, cozy and comfortable, in the dark. I begin to tally up. *What does it all mean? Ha, a dangerous question.* Drinking single-malt scotch, I listen to the furnace and the refrigerator making their gentle winter noises. The furnace stops, then the fridge—complete silence.

The small shine of light on the snow from the window above quits, so I know Beth has put her book away and is going to sleep. She likes to get an early start in the morning, but I wish she would make time for me. It's been a while. She has her schedule—a busy life with the house, her girlfriends, and her volunteer work.

I do have reason to celebrate. I'm feeling smug because I'm, we're, a half a million dollars richer. For commemoration and R&R, I've squeezed out a ten-day vacation at a plush hotel with reef diving. Today, in superior court, a fine jury awarded my client and his family one and a half million dollars for a car accident. Considering what he went through, his permanent injuries, and the negligence of the drunk driver, the award was right in the ballpark. My share is one-third, the standard fee. This is the ninth amount of over one mil I've earned for my clients, and these cases alone have made me rich. My reputation and that of the firm in which I am a partner brings me good cases. I bust my ass, and I usually force my opponents to settle for big bucks. Otherwise, like today, they face a jury that might award more.

Although I should be happy and satisfied this evening, I'm filled with melancholy. I've experienced post-award letdown before, but I've never felt quite this empty. I seldom reminisce, because it's looking backward. And when I do indulge myself in remembrances, I think of the years when Beth and I were first married and when our daughter was young. Then there are old torts, won and lost. I give my profession everything I can. It's where my psyche resides. Tonight, however, is the hot summer of my discontent. Moon shadows on the snow have me longing to melt everything away. I wish for warmer seasons, warmer company. I recall my youth, and I'm back on campus, studying law.

In addition to recreating in the VW, Diana majored in anthropology with a minor in French—two rather unproductive domains of learning, at least vocationally.

"Where you going with anthro and French, anyway? What can you do with them?" We were on the sidewalk, leaving the law library after a long evening study session. It was one of the few times I inquired about her future plans, and it was part of a larger conversation. She was telling me that she had spent a summer and a semester studying and traveling in Europe and that it gave her a broader outlook. Perhaps intellectually she had come up to my level, but her interests were unfocused and less practical. It seemed to me she didn't have a clue as to what she wanted to do in life, and she had said she didn't want to teach and she had no interest in graduate school.

"Something will come to me. Not everyone has their life all worked out, like you. I want to start living. I feel like I'm perpetually preparing."

The fact that Diana had a car and I didn't meant that we either met somewhere on campus or she collected me at my apartment. One thing she avoided was having me meet her at the dorm, because she knew this would set me off. I had had it with group living and lived in a four-person apartment only because I had to. Eventually, though, there came a day when it was more convenient for both of us that I call for her at the dorm. Just walking up the steps to the dormitory ticked me off. I swung open the big, heavy institutional doors, and they closed behind me. My shoes scraped and slid across the smooth, hard floor. I ruminated that dormitories were for freshmen, still green teenagers, large children with cheery undergraduate faces who pulled tricks on each other. At the reception desk, the student-desk clerk asked me whom I wanted to page.

"Diana in 324." I felt like a freshman again, an irritating demotion for a second-year, almost third-year, law student.

"Hello, wall," Diana's roommate said, laughing at the intercom. This was the Age of Aquarius, and Diana was living in a female-segregated dorm in which, by rule, no men were allowed on the floors, period. Most dorms by then had gone coed at least by floor.

I sulked on a chrome-framed vinyl chair until she came down. Once we were outside, I complained that she ought to live in an apartment. We were too sophisticated for this confining lifestyle.

She said she could meet elsewhere if I wanted, and explained defensively, "The dorm takes care of me; don't you understand?"

My face lacked sympathy, so she told me more, whether I wanted to hear it or not.

"I don't have to clean the bathroom or scrub the kitchen floor. The food is cooked for me, and I don't have to figure out what to buy at the grocery. I can eat with people in the cafeteria or sit alone. It's safe, utilities are paid, and it wraps me in a snug cocoon."

What a quaint outlook on life, much different from mine. I wanted nothing to wrap me up and no one to take care of me. I could do just fine. I wanted independence, freedom, and efficiency.

Perhaps Diana's outlook was influenced by her family's disintegration. Soon after she left for college, her parents divorced and her father remarried. Then he got pancreatic cancer and died before her junior year. Diana wasn't close to her mother, who by then had moved to Arizona.

"I never call her at night because she is always tipsy and starts crying," Diana once confided. A wild sister moved to LA and didn't answer letters or calls. Her collapsed family could drive Diana into the dumps, but it never hurt her grades. *I suppose I should give her credit for keeping steady after all of her family moorings slipped.* In ways different from me, she was just as strong.

Diana, who had been active in high school— majorette, clarinet, school paper, and athletics—limited herself now to studying, yoga, and exercise. She was well organized as people go, but I sensed an emotional void. A good man might save her from existential despair.

One begins to feel there is a kind and compassionate God when one's three college apartment sharers, including one's roommate, leave for the weekend. Despair, existential or otherwise, is out of the question when you and your girlfriend get to play house for two nights and days. It sure beat the hell out of the claustrophobic Volkswagen. Still, studying came first. We sat across from each other at the kitchen table for long study sessions, and when that was over, we played the stereo, relaxed, and drank cheap apple wine, which we called Chateau de Boone. From Diana's reaction to the notion of having our own place, I wondered, again, how she could stand living in the dorm. She worked the kitchen as if it were her own and, in my mind's palate, created the best lasagna ever.

On Sunday morning, I ran down to the corner and got the *New York Times*. We spread it over the two beds, now scrunched together as one big bed. I read the Week in Review while she read the travel section. We knew we had just the morning remaining before one or more of the guys returned. Apartment heat turned up, sitting in our underwear and drinking coffee, both of us were feeling loose, but at the same time, we were hyped up with caffeine and the domestic situation. She started stretching and got up and walked back and forth; then she did a cartwheel in the space vacated by the moved bed.

I looked up from the paper. "If you can do a handstand, I'll nominate you for centerfold of the year."

She plopped on the bed and smiled. "No sweat." She unhooked her bra and tossed it to me. Then she did a handstand from the elbows, long hair falling, ample breasts more perfect in reverse gravity. I held my breath. Then she dropped down to her back and propped herself up in a bicycle exercise pose. I was paralyzed, dumbfounded. She looked into my eyes, giggled, and winked. Then she rolled over and kissed me hard, tongue just brushing my lips. After thirty years, my chest rises and my head lightens.

I wish Beth would have … Maybe I should have rubbed her back for a while. Allowing for normal aging, Beth is as pretty now as when I met her. She is still a thin, tight-muscled trophy. She does aerobics at her gym or walks most days. Other times she uses our assortment of stair-step, skiing, and weight machines collected in our basement exercise room. She is a born attorney's wife—alert, socially aggressive, polished, and proper. She serves on committees, devotes time to charities, and puts style into everything she does. Our home is decorated like a magazine spread. I've made as many contacts in the community through her activities as I have through my work. We play bridge and golf at the best country club. Without her, I become dull and absorbed by my practice. Still, I feel there's something lacking. We rarely touch. We sleep on the far sides of a king-size bed and never snuggle. Do people still snuggle? Perhaps just young people.

When I met Beth, I knew immediately that she could help me achieve the lifestyle, and she knew it too. Soon after we started dating, we had a meeting of the minds and a blazing physical relationship. It was different than it had been with Diana. In retrospect, it seems like a stage Beth and I had to go through.

She was a foxy sorority sister, a senior, and I was in my third and last year of law school. After I passed the bar exam and started with a good law firm, we married in a very tasteful ceremony in her hometown. Pretty quickly after that, it seemed, we became an old married couple, and in remarkably few years we settled into American normalcy. Our sex became an exercise in marital relations, health, and duty. It has been virtually scheduled—once a week, less sensual, without emotional connection.

Just before our daughter's third birthday, Beth had a miscarriage. She was devastated and didn't want to go through it again. Also, about that time, I started making so much money that it made sense for Beth to give up teaching. She devoted herself to being an attorney's family partner. She wanted to be a good mother, keep a beautiful house, and be active in the church and community. We also began to entertain often, and we became involved in local politics.

Poverty in college makes you appreciate later affluence, and keeping body and soul together at law school wasn't easy. Much of my tuition was paid with scholarships, and I had part-time jobs. My parents gave me money, and I had loans, but altogether, I was still in college poverty. I didn't want to work much, because I needed to study to stay at the top level of my class. On occasion, though, I was open to other schemes.

One of the ways I kept myself in pocket money was to sneak into the golf course and dive for lost golf balls in Lake Scarlet. Calling this extra-large golf club pond a lake was a considerable promotion. There were other water hazards on the course, but Scarlet received the most balls. With a robust stand of pine trees on one end, it bordered two fairways and the green of the seventh hole. It was always chock full of balls.

"My handicap is Lake Scarlet," was a common duffer's lament. When my old diving buddy graduated, I brought Diana in as a new partner. She had a car.

It was easy to sneak onto the course at night. There was an all-night caretaker, but he stayed up near the clubhouse and the other buildings. At dusk he made a course run in a golf cart to make sure everyone was off. He might come out again if he heard something or felt like a late ride, but he rarely came out after dark. On Sunday nights, the routine was the same, and even the restaurant closed up after ten or so.

Scarlet was the most prestigious course in the region, designed by a famous architect for beauty and difficulty. Its golfers were affluent and used the best balls, which were easy to sell to the public golf course and the driving ranges. A good night's work netted what was, for college kids, big money, and the danger of getting caught made it an adventure.

We parked the VW off the road, half in the ditch, on a side drive leading from a farm. Then we walked less than a quarter mile to the course and down to the pond at the end of the fairway behind and to the right side of the green. The open fairways seemed bright, so we made our way without flashlights. Sunday nights closest to a full moon were the ideal times for our enterprise. Often Scarlet was half carpeted with errant, dimpled, spherical eggs before groundskeepers would dredge the pond with nets on long poles.

As the moon rose to its highest, we began to fill two mesh divers' bags with the balls and haul them to shore to pour into an old canvas duffle bag rigged up on a golf cart. With bags over shoulders and the full cart, one trip back to the car was about all we could risk because of the noise.

At midnight, it was still hot, maybe ninety degrees, but it felt like a hundred with the humidity. By the time Diana and I walked to the pond, we were both wet through our T-shirts. We stripped to our swimsuits, and I got the bags ready. She put on her fins and snorkel ahead of me and waded out and dove in. I was taking a long time, making sure the duffel bag was secure on the cart. She splashed at me and whispered loudly, "Come on." I waved her off. A few seconds later she slung the top of her bathing suit at me and it whipped across my chest and flipped away.

In the dim light, I followed her into the tepid pond. Like two night-stealing otters glistening in the moonlight, we dove. Of course, the depth never exceeded eight feet, even in the middle. Where it was that deep, we felt for the balls in the darker water. Bluegills nibbled at our sides, and catfish and crayfish moved away as we harvested. Visibility in the amber-tinted water was good with the high, angled moonlight. Diana's untanned breasts glowed. As she treaded water, they buoyed up and jiggled. She swam, and I swam under her. I was the Creature from the Black Lagoon, a voyeur below, moonstruck by each silhouetted arm stoke.

It wasn't easy, but I forced myself back to the job at hand. This was business; I needed the money, and so did she. We had to be quiet and quick. After forty minutes of collecting balls, our mesh bags needed emptying for the second time. I towed them back to the shore and transferred their contents, filling the duffel bag to about three-quarters full. One more load each and we'd be out of there.

We had finished the side touching the dogleg fairway. There were more here than on the side touching the green, or the far side against the rough. We filled our bags with all we could manage and started back to our entry point.

"What's that?" Diana had heard before I did the rattle of the caretaker's power cart bouncing over the fairway. I saw it had no lights, but the caretaker shined a flashlight. He was still a long way off, and tall vegetation blocked his vision of the pond. I got over to our cart and pulled everything, clothes and all, into deep water. We slipped over to the reeds and lily pads and kept our faces behind cover.

At the edge of the pond, a little farther off from where the packs had been, the caretaker braked to a stop. He shined his light on the ground and bent down, not getting out of the driver's seat. The packs were gone. *I took everything*, I thought. *What is he doing?*

"He's found my top," Diana whispered. The caretaker held up the bikini top like unidentified roadkill. He shined the light up and down on his prize and then passed the long ray of light over the pond. We ducked before his light reached the reeds. He swept it back and forth, but we stayed down. Then he gave up and drove down the cart track to the tenth hole. A routine night check—maybe to cool off, we guessed. It was still hot; the surface water temperature was as warm as the air. We went back to the shore, but Diana's bikini top was gone. Finders keepers? A trophy for the caretaker? An item to pin up on the lost-and-found bulletin board? We worried that he might double back, but we began to pull our things off the bottom. Then we thought we heard something and returned to the reeds. It was nothing, and we decided the caretaker was gone for good.

I stood in the chest-deep water just outside the reeds. When I turned back to look for her, she gave me a kiss, and I pulled her into me. A kiss in the warm water. I felt her buoyant, soft boobs against my chest. I moved her suit aside, and she wrapped her legs around me, still with fins on her feet. She was softness, moisture, and response.

Oh yes, and I have to laugh. On the way out, rolling our loot on the golf cart, we came across a new sight around the front edge of the pond. In the faint light, we could just make out a big red warning sign that threatened,

Any persons (except players) caught
collecting golf balls on this course will be
prosecuted and have their balls removed.

"You'd better get out of here quick, sonny boy!" Diana said, and she snapped a towel low toward me.

We never went back to Lake Scarlet, but not because of the sign. We just never did it again, and I never took anyone else after that.

"There's no romance in a hometown girl," my uncle, an attorney who married a woman from Toronto, once advised me. I knew what he meant. There's less mystery with too many common experiences. Although we didn't date until college, Diana was from my own high school, and we knew all about each other. This was part of the problem with her, but not all of it. We were still together in the fall, a long time for me. I was beginning to worry about her getting pregnant. She said she had gotten birth control pills from Planned Parenthood, but would she mess them up? Did the pills work all the time? She was graduating in December, and I had another year and a half of law school, then several months studying for the bar exam. I was focused on law school and becoming a lawyer, not much else.

"What do you think I should do in January?" Diana interrupted our studying to ask this, and I did not respond, so she asked it a second time.

"I don't know. What do you do with a degree in anthropology? Must be something."

I was thinking, *How many BS anthropologists get jobs in their major? Four or five in the US, I'll bet. Graduate school openings are few, and what can you do outside of the university with a degree in anthropology*? I couldn't tell her what to do. It seemed she had no options.

"Help me to decide. You always know what to do."

"I can't. I don't know your field." On some level, I knew what she wanted, but I acted as if I didn't. I treated each discussion on her future superficially, as if it were just her future we were talking about. She wanted to know if she should plan to stay in town while I finished law school. Her life was at loose ends without school. It would make sense if she could define her life by mine.

I could have done worse. I didn't doubt her love for me and our physical lovemaking would be hard to give up. But more than that, our relationship was comfortable. I've always been an antsy guy, and I could feel at ease with Diana. Sometimes, we could just sit and watch the river flow. But ease and contentment were not what I was looking for.

The fall warmth continued through November and the late football season. It was impossible not to be affected by mania of the big last game. Streets were blocked, and the town and the campus devoted itself to the Saturday spectacle. Although we were marginal fans, we had the game on the radio in her VW, which was parked down by the river. We thought we should listen, but we grew bored with the game and got out for a walk on the riverbank trail.

"Do you think you'll ever get married?" she asked. The question was too direct, I thought. I had never told her that I loved her.

"I don't know. I just want to concentrate one hundred percent on law school, and I'll worry about the rest of my life later. The law is everything to me. I feel like I was born to be an attorney. Both the profession and the lifestyle suit me to the max, and I want to be the best lawyer I can be."

She did not reply for a long time. I didn't mean it as a rebuff, but I gave away more than I knew. The implications were more apparent to her than to me. For one thing, it meant that I had not thought of marrying her. She did not press me. Perhaps she divined from my few remarks what I didn't say, that she was not in a class or set of persons from which I might choose a wife.

I didn't let myself work out her side of it. I was aware at some level that she might take it as rejection, but I hoped that she would not big-deal it. I still wanted to go on seeing her. I wanted our relationship to continue as it had. Maybe I wanted her to wear me down. I had not thought it out. Her question was a prompt to start thinking, but I ignored it. Was this fair to her, not thinking about our romantic future? She acted on it, fair or not.

"I'm flying out to visit my mother over Thanksgiving, and you're going home. So let's cool it for a week or so. I know you have a lot to do. We're both busy."

"Okay. Finals are coming up. Let's do that." I appreciated an out from the earlier topic.

On Thursday, after Thanksgiving, I called her. She said she had an interview for a full-time staff job with the university and that she was arranging to move into an apartment with a girlfriend. She could not go out that weekend. Maybe none of this was true. She was working out the details of something else. I objected about not going out, but I had so much studying to do that I was somewhat relieved.

I called her again on the following Tuesday, after a test. She said she had had a good interview with the university and that her apartment hunting was still continuing. I asked to see her, and she said she was too busy with graduation stuff and moving. Then she said, "You know, I don't want to waste my love on somebody who doesn't value it, doesn't love me."

"I do value it! Please don't pressure me. Why do we have to do this during exams? We can postpone this conversation."

She waited before answering. It was hard to tell what she was thinking on the phone, but she seemed to come to some decision. "Okay. Let's not see each other until the weekend, to give both of us some time to think."

I sensed this had some sort a catch, an on-off indicator for her, but I agreed anyway. I was worried about one of my exams, and I wanted to concentrate. *We can work this out later.* Or so I thought.

When I went over to her dorm Friday, no one answered the intercom in her room, and no one answered the telephone that night. On Saturday, her roommate answered the phone and said Diana was out and she didn't know where. I told her that I had been taking finals all week and that I wanted to catch up. I wanted to know what she was doing for graduation.

Her roommate revealed that Diana was gone; she had taken all her clothes and belongings and didn't even say good-bye. "I really don't know where she went."

Beginning to panic, I called several university offices to see if I could get any information; I drew a blank. What the hell was she doing? What kind of irrational stunt was this? My first concern was from my own perspective, not at all from hers. I was afraid she might have driven her Beetle off a bridge, or locked herself in a garage with the motor running, or maybe she was lurking outside my apartment, waiting to stab me. She must have lost it. What was she up to? I ran through all of the alternatives, but I missed the one she chose. If Diana were a man, what she did wouldn't have been surprising.

I decided to try her roommate again. *She might be holding out on me.* I called her and told her I was going to call Diana's mother in Arizona—and maybe the police.

The roommate finally broke down. "Look, I promised not to tell you, but Diana enlisted in the army for officer training school. She left on a bus Friday, the day after her last final, and she's skipping graduation ceremonies. That's all I know, I swear, except that the army promised her Vietnamese language training."

How very patriotic. I couldn't believe it. What an insult. Diana's enlistment was something like taking sisterly vows. She had become the bride of Uncle Sam. The army was taking care of her instead of college and the dorm, instead of me. She had given up her life to the army, and all her needs would be fulfilled. Was my churlish lack of love so easily surrogated? There was nothing I could do. She meant it to be irrevocable—like death, like suicide.

As the century turns, if she is alive, Diana has reached middle age. She must have married. She could be divorced. She may have adult children, even a big family. I could turn on my computer and try to find traces of her. Perhaps she has led a more adventurous life than I. Of course, she has changed. She could be fat and ugly, although I doubt she'd allow that. She may have had a wonderful life, or she may have been disappointed. Maybe the university has—

No. I would not like to see her or even know about her life. I'll remember her as perfect. She'll always be strong and soft, warm and vulnerable, loving me more than she should, with moonlit breasts buoyed up by amber waters.

Broken-Bat Single

JOHNNY "BIG BAT" HARKER SNAPPED THE BOOK SHUT. "Wow! Scary, man. Gets in your head." He said it out loud, although there was no one else in the room. Then he took a slug from his fourth can of beer. The nickname Big Bat referred to his professional baseball career, but right now Johnny was struggling through a novel his wife, Mina, had read. He wanted to get back, as he would say it, on his fine babe's wavelength 'cause she was bitching him down all the time. Johnny shrugged as he reviewed the situation. *What can I say? She is always right.* He still loved her, or at least loved the way she used to be, but this, his second marriage, was going down the tubes. Last night she went off at him with her big mouth, and he went a little nuts. He smacked her once, not hard, and pushed her down in bed. He felt bad that her eye puffed up a little.

Johnny had pulled the novel off of Mina's shelf of books. She liked movie and TV vampires and read about them too. Usually, Johnny didn't have time to read much more than the sports section of the newspaper. Except for a couple of *Sports Illustrated Baseball All-Star Review* editions, all the books in the house were hers. *Dracula*, Bram Stoker's work, was the only one he recognized. The others had weird titles, like *Dark Thirst* and *Twilight Forever*. He thought that if he could get into one of these vampire books, he might have something to talk about with her. But he had been reading for several days now, and the book was messin' with his mind. He woke up last night, clenching his teeth and hissing into the dark, apparently trying to out-Drac Dracula, competitive as he was. His recollection of the dream wasn't too clear. Johnnie's thinking in general, never a highlight of his persona, had become a little blurry in the last year or so, which didn't help his marriage either.

Johnny Big Bat, a fan favorite, picked at a new zit that had emerged under the corner of his jaw. He popped it with his finger and thumb nails, and his shoulders shivered involuntarily with the pain. He wiped away the blood with his hand and blotted behind the right knee of his Phat Farm jeans. He had a bunch of zits on his back too. These, along with a back brace for a cracked vertebra, made him uncomfortable as he read from a reclined position in his leather La-Z-Boy, heat and massage model. *Thirty-eight is too old for zits*, he thought to himself, *but it's the price you pay for being so masculine.*

"Damn," he said, again to no one. He was late tuning in the TV to watch the game. Joining it at the top of the third, he watched his teammates, the Angels, struggle in a pitchers' duel with the Rays in Anaheim.

Johnny hated it when the pitchers sucked all the life out of the game. Slugfests were what he wanted—both teams in double digits. "Who kicked the extra points," he liked to say about the high-scoring games. It was just killing Johnny to be home alone as his team played the last game of the season. A utility player who couldn't hit a good curve ball if the catcher told him it was coming was playing Johnny's position, first base. Poor Johnny was out of baseball for the first time in twenty years.

Johnny wasn't quite alone at home, although the household help had left three hours ago. Mina was asleep in the master bedroom upstairs. His kid lived with his first wife. So far, wife number two, a former first-runner-up for Miss New Jersey, hadn't gotten knocked up—not that they hadn't worked at it. But actually, when he was trying to be honest with himself, he would admit to being mostly disinterested, which he attributed to Major League pressure.

The Angels tied the score in the fifth with a walk, an advance on a fielder's choice, a stolen base, and a sacrifice fly.

"A run with no hits? Fuck that!" Johnny shouted at the TV, and he ran his hand over his shaved head. "This is baseball?" he said for posterity. "Let's see some fucking hits!" By now he was used to the looks of his shiny cranium, but when he felt the raised stubble low on the back side, he got the willies, just as much as he did when he first shaved it off months ago. His hairline had retreated north recently, too far for a comb-over to look good. He told himself he would have to take his ball cap off sometime, so he shaved his head clean as a tangerine. He thought it looked manly and tough, which seemed more important to him than it used to. It went with his big muscles and aggressive attitude.

Johnny yearned to get back in the game and felt he had lost his importance. He was always at loose ends in the off-season, but this off-season was the most important of his career. He had to heal up and gain more strength for his final seasons and the push for his place in home run history. He could feel that record-breaking home run yet to come. His hands would sting when he blasted the ball on what a sports writer once called "an impossible parabola." The crowd would sigh loudly in awe at the crack of the bat and as the small white dot went up. They would cheer as it came down. Maybe it would clear the stadium entirely over center field and bounce around the buses in the parking lot with kids scrambling to grab it. He would round the bases and tip his hat once again.

Pfissffff! Johnny pulled the tab on his fifth beer and wondered if maybe he had heard his last cheer from the crowd. He began to mope on the couch, watching the game, feeling, imagining his future disappointment. In the sixth inning of the TV game, he winced as a big right-hander, going for the fences, took a maximum swing, twisting his torso, bringing the bat around in full circle, and missing the ball entirely. It was a similar swing that had ended Johnny's season. A vertebra cracked, and from then on, pain was his constant companion. Luckily, his injury came late in the season and he had the off-season to recover. It was okay. His team was out of the playoffs anyway. "Cheers to that," he said, and he chugged half of his beer.

With time, his vertebrae would heal. The pain had already subsided somewhat with the medication. He hoped that he would be restored enough by March to join his team in spring training. Leaving baseball would be the death of him. He was still in his thirties and thirty-fifth on the all-time home run record, right behind Jeff Bagwell, with 448 dingers. He was on the verge of becoming a superstar, and he could be washed up. Being idle had affected his mental health and made him anxious and even a little paranoid. The loss of his calling—the thing he had trained for all his life, the thing that had occupied most of his thoughts every day of the year—was driving him nuts. He chugged the rest of his beer and got a new one.

Then there was the beautiful Mina. She dug being a Major League wife, and she kept herself in Major League condition, too. She got a lot of attention when she sunned in her bikini by the pool during spring training. Attached to his arm in public, she made him look like a king. Would she still love him as a has-been? What was the trouble? They had scads of money—tens of millions. If they divorced, half at least would be hers—this was California. But it wasn't the money. He feared that it was his celebrity she loved.

After the game on TV was finished, he read for ten minutes, and then his concentration waned. He nodded off and began to dream of the book again. Then he awoke and cried out softly. He staggered forward, clutching the table, staring with glazed eyes, and gasping with an open mouth. Something urged him to the window and compelled him to scan his backyard for … for … he didn't know what. The darkness was eerie to him; not a cricket chirped, and the distant dog that barked nearly every night was mute. The warm, clear evening had turned cooler, more humid, and murky with fog. Leaves hung motionless in the dead air. Johnny scratched his left nipple, which was wet and a little swollen. He slid aside the door screen and stepped out on his tiled patio. The quiet put him on guard. Why? He looked from one side of the yard to the other. As he turned to go back in, he thought he saw a flutter at the north end of the house, near the roof on the second floor. A few wing flaps shuffled lightly in the still air. *Is it a bat? If that's what it is, it's a big one.* He told himself it was nothing—or, in any event, that it meant nothing. After returning and sliding back the screen, he picked up his book but stood listening.

Johnny had developed a phobia about prowlers. He thought of getting the gun they kept in the house, but Mina had taken to keeping it in her bedroom nightstand drawer for safety. (She said she was worried about being alone when he was on the road or when he had night games.) So he retrieved from the front closet his old ash baseball bat, a Louisville Slugger 36, Jackie Robinson Special. It was his favorite bat, a bat suitable for the Babe to swat a deep one over the fence in Yankee Stadium. Johnny kept it around just in case there were prowlers, but they hadn't had any so far. With his new temper, he didn't quite trust himself with the gun anyway.

He sat back in his chair and the lamp shone down on him in the otherwise dark room. His reading concentration wavered. His heart beat faster, and his breathing quickened. He stood and looked out of the window again. Nothing had changed. Behind him was a sound of breathing out, a sigh or a hiss, barely audible. He turned; there was nothing. He walked quickly from the dining room, through the entryway, to the front door. It was locked and chained from the inside. He had been sitting by the back door, and his reading chair was in sight of the locked door to the garage. Nothing had come through these entryways. On the lower floor, the kitchen, dining room, living room, and every other room was as it should be. By the process of elimination, he figured that the threat was on the floor above; or below, in the basement. He could feel it now. *It's upstairs, where Mina is sleeping!* The dark presence was there!

Bounding up three steps at a time, he arrived at the upstairs landing with his heart pounding. There were no signs of any intrusions in the extra bedrooms, the guestroom, or the bathroom. The hallway was empty. Passing each room, he looked in, flicking the lights on, then off. Outside the master bedroom door, he stopped. There was no golden stream of light on the floor beneath the closed door. It was his wife's custom to read for a while in bed before sleeping. Should he open the door? She might get mad if he woke her up for no reason. He had been sleeping in the guest bedroom since he hurt his back. Still he felt compelled check on her tonight.

Johnny felt a sixth sense magnifying his perceptions as he opened the door. Wickedness seemed to ooze out as the gap widened. Johnny's eyes adjusted to the dark, and he made out a huge body draped over his beautiful wife. A monster had attached itself to her neck! Johnny could see it all. It was as if he were starring in a movie.

Engrossed in its blood passion, the creature was not alerted by Johnny's quiet entrance, but it sensed his closer approach and rose up, startled, seeing elbows and a bat cocked for action. Johnny struck the hair-slicked-back head of the intruder with a swing that would have homered over the Green Monster in Fenway Park. There was a large crack. The slam should have separated the thing's head from its shoulders. Instead, the head did not move or give way. Johnny felt as though he had hit a statue or the side of a building.

The bizarre trespasser turned fiercely, eyes wide, teeth gleaming. It did not seem to be in pain, but greatly affronted. The fiend rose to meet the challenger. It seemed much larger than Johnny's six-foot-three frame.

Johnny gasped at the mirror of his wife's vanity table. In the reflection, he was alone with his wife, no invader threatening. The tall brute cast its burning eyes on him. Johnny's mind was seized in a hypnotic bind, but with all of his Major League will, he shook it off, concentrating on defeating the evil menace in his bedroom. Johnny struck the repulsive thing again with a flat blow that could have sent a line drive bouncing off the fence for a triple. Once again, he experienced the shock of hitting an immovable object. The creature's head and shoulders remained stiffly unaffected. Then it snarled and raised its arms and groped as Johnny struck again. With a force that would break a steel table leg, the bat struck a weirdly cloaked arm offered up in defense. But the arm did not give; it was the bat that broke, sharply splintering as if it had hit a fastball on the trademark. Johnny was left holding the sharply splintered handle and shank, while the barrel flew off, striking the window casing.

Sneering and rolling his r's, Dracula told him, "Strike three, you're out."

Johnny saw it move to embrace him. Unafraid, he taunted, "All right, come on, you decrepit, snaggle-toothed switch-hitter. Hit me with your best shot!"

Enraged, Dracula threw himself at his prey. Johnny met the monster's rush with a lunge of his own. The man and demon collided at the foot of the bed, but it was the stronger, larger intruder who fell back—in yet another violation of natural and physical law. In its chest, between two ribs, the sharp shank of the broken bat handle had been thrust deep into its heart. As the fanged monster staggered back, Johnny shoved the knob deeper, and he kicked it until the broken end penetrated through the back ribs to the outside. The vampire fell to its knees, clutching its chest, head rearing back, teeth gnashing.

"No, I'm safe," Johnny jeered at the gnarled figure

in its moribund struggles. "And your season's over, batboy. You didn't make the playoffs."

Then the monstrosity turned and fell, flat-faced, on the floor, driving the stake in as far as it could go, up to the hilt of the knob. With a flash and a sizzle, the specter was reduced to ash, and then the ash vanished, leaving no trace, not even a spot on the carpet.

Johnny heard a cricket start up its rhythmic chirp outside in the grass. In the distance, the dog barked. He heard Mina turn and breathe a sigh in her sleep, and they were alone in the night.

Mina rolled over to the far edge of their California king bed and turned on the lamp. She blinked in the light and focused on Johnny. Then, from the nightstand drawer, she pulled out the snub-nosed .38 that she kept there for safety. Johnny's head began to clear when he realized Mina was pointing the gun at him.

"Are you done?" Mina demanded. "Are you done prancing around with that bat? You lack-love, limp-dicked loser, you broke the door frame! Are you crazy? Look at what you did." She pulled the top of her negligee together with her free hand.

Johnny noticed that last night's red mark beside her left eye had developed into a shiner. He looked around the room. The counter of Mina's dresser had been lifted off from a blow below. Her cosmetics, photos, and other things had been slung around the room. There was a hole in the wall, a window was broken, and the doorframe was off, bashed in and entirely broken away from one side of the door.

"Are you going to kill me now?" Mina said. "Should I say my prayers? What now? What now? Say something."

Bewildered, he had no answer. He then sputtered out, "I killed Dracula." Johnny looked at her for understanding. "He was on you. I thought … I thought he was drainin' you."

"You thought … How did your hot, roasted brain come up with that shit?" She picked up the phone and dialed 911 right as Johnny was watching, dumbfounded. She kept the gun pointed in his direction even as she dialed.

"I was reading it, and it must have made me dream," Johnny finally got out.

"Hallucinate! Not a dream. The word is 'hallucinate'! You crazy bastard! This is the last straw. If you think Dracula was a bloodsucker, wait until you see my divorce settlement. I got a whole firm of jackal-assed lawyers who will pick your bones clean." There was an answer on the phone. "Hello, 911?" Mina greeted, "This is Mina Harker. My husband, Johnny Big Bat Harker, just went berserk breaking up the house with a bat. I think he might try to kill me. Yes he's right here in the bedroom, but I think he's leaving." She looked up at Johnny. "You are you leaving! Go over to your sorry-ass trainer's house. Beat his door with a bat. I told you to get offa that shit. Go check into rehab, but don't come crawling back here, you dumb motherfucker."

She said into the phone, "Yes, Officer, come over quickly. I'll press charges. Please hurry. I don't know what he'll do."

Refocusing on Johnny, Mina pulled back the pistol's hammer and ordered loudly, "Get out of here. Now! The cops are coming."

Johnny felt her fiery eyes were scarier than Dracula's. He turned to leave.

"Sure you don't want to leave another mark on me before you go?" Mina turned her shiner up to him. She had a lot of nerve.

Johnny Big Bat hung his head and shook it. "No. I'm leaving." He went downstairs straight to the garage and drove out into the night, looking for a place to sleep.

Who Ripped Off My Lunch?

(A Short Contemporary Mystery)

"WHO RIPPED OFF MY LUNCH?"

He searched the cruddy back corners of the lunchroom refrigerator. The one bag he thought might have been his was all wrong. This morning he packed a salami-and-monterey-jack Lunchables meal, a cup of blueberry yogurt with a spoon, a can of V8, and a banana—a recognizable lunch. Only he could have made it. No one could have mistaken it. It was a man's lunch—nothing prepared, just a bunch of stuff chucked into a bag. Because he was especially hungry, he was ready to make trouble over his loss. Someone in this building was eating his chilled banquet, and he was going to find the filcher.

In a quick tour of the break room and the mazes of hallways winding past open offices, he found no incriminating discarded Lunchables pack. He sniffed out no telltale odor of salami or banana. However, he came across a nice staff potluck in the break room near another set of offices at the other end of the building.

He knew some of the people there, and they were gracious enough to invite him in to share sloppy joes, homemade soup, au gratin potatoes, three interesting salads, and several wonderful desserts. Best of all, there was good conversation. This was much better than peeling open a Lunchables pack alone in his office. *Thank you, lunch thief, whoever you are.*

At home during dinner, Younger Son complained to his mother that she put a banana in his lunch. "You know I hate bananas."

Father asked Mother, "Did you put a Juicy Juice box, potato salad, coleslaw, and a ham sandwich in his lunch?"

"Yes."

At noon, he had noticed a lunch like this in the office refrigerator. He also remembered driving Younger Son to school that morning and seeing two brown bags sitting together in the space between the bucket seats.

The Man Who Didn't Care

"HERE YOU GO." THE GUARD TOSSED HIM THE *DETROIT Free Press* like a bone to a dog. "Front page." The guard walked away, smiling.

Frank was miffed that his name wasn't in the banner headline, "Michigan's First Execution Scheduled Today." It was six in the morning. The event was scheduled for eleven. Sitting on the bed, he looked at his story for a while but decided there was nothing new. Then he rubbed his sleepy eyes and pulled out the sports section, pushing the rest of the paper away.

His eight-by-ten cell was almost heavenly. Walls, ceiling, bars, bed, cotton blanket, all white. Floor was light grey. The stainless steel toilet and the sink above and behind it shared a covered water intake. The bed had three open compartments built in below it, two small and one big. He could have hygiene items, two appliances, two books, and writing materials. There was a small desk surface, painted white, attached to the wall at standing height. He had never used it.

Last night they had let him have anything he wanted

for dinner. It was three cheeseburgers, double fries, apple pie, and a chocolate milkshake; but technically this morning was his last meal. Breakfast arrived on a cart, and a table was set up before him. Guards watched him closely. He got a plastic spork.

Like dinner, his last breakfast wasn't that special. He had three eggs over easy; four slices of ham, which he cut with edge of his utensil with practiced skill; a dozen pieces of bacon; a pile of home fries; white toast; and coffee. He put a lot of ketchup on the eggs and potatoes and washed it all down with another chocolate shake. Then he smoked a cigarette. He thought about ordering other things, but he was stuffed. They wouldn't get him a six-pack of Budweiser.

They did offer him a Valium. Not being a man who declined interesting substances, he took it and asked, "Hey, how about a couple more?" But they told him he could have only one. Wasn't allowed to go out all buzzed up. It was okay. He really didn't care.

He took up the sports section again. The main story was about the ongoing Red Wings winning streak and how excited everyone was—looked like they were on the way to another Stanley Cup. The Pistons had dropped another one, but that was no big deal. *Those losers will have to work to make the playoffs, and then they'll get knocked off quickly.* The story was jumped to an inside page. He finished it and then looked at the statistics and standings for hockey and basketball. The next page was nonsports and ads. His eyes swept to the bottom, and he focused on a short filler with the headline "Late-Term

Abortions on the Rise in Michigan." He chuckled softly twice, then cleared his throat. He tossed the sports section over on top of the rest of the paper.

A little bit of sports news was about the extent of his reading. More was unnecessary, usually. It was work, and it reminded him of his failures in school, which he had dropped out of in tenth grade. A year later, they started him up on a GED at the juvie center, but he dropped that as soon as he got out. You couldn't really call him stupid, because he could figure out what he had to. He just didn't care about more than that. One thing he prided himself on, though: he always got even when somebody crossed him.

Gee, a Bud or even a Busch would taste really good right now. When he wasn't incarcerated, Frank drank when he could, keeping a low buzz going most of the time. He drank alone, generally, but he would party when there was an opportunity, especially if someone else was buying. He had a short history of drug dealing but wasn't up to the business end of it. Also, it was kind of dangerous. He was almost busted with inventory once and had to flush a bunch of crack down the toilet. Then he couldn't make up the difference with his supplier. He was lucky to have just had the hell beaten out of him. During that time, he became addicted himself and went to prison after being caught in a B and E to support his habit. He got over addiction in prison, and after that he kept off the hard stuff most of the time. He didn't want it on his mind so much. Still, he smoked pot or drank several or more beers every day.

During his first sentence, to relieve the boredom, he started working out with weights. At five feet eight he felt he had to be extra strong. He was always tough, and he grew to count on his strength. Unwanted and abused as a child by the many temporary men of the household, he never met his father and he could never count on his mother or his assorted half-siblings. By now his mother was probably dead, and anyway, no one visited him in prison. A jack of a hundred short-term jobs, he was thirty-six but looked older. Prison life and his circumstances had given his light-skinned face a dour cast, which was accented by his dark eyes and hair.

Frank-in-short-chains made the long walk down to the execution chamber with no problems. The prison chaplain walked with him. Frank didn't care about Jesus, but it was easier for him to say, "Yes, I have," when asked if he had accepted Christ as his savior. There were just a few prisoners on the hastily converted death row in Jackson State Prison. Each acknowledged him as he passed.

One waved and said, "God bless you."

Another said, "Show them how it's done."

The last added, "Don't worry, Frank; they can kill ya, but they can't eat ya," and laughed.

"Crazy fucking asshole," Frank fired back at him. "You're next, motherfucker!"

Michigan was the first state to outlaw capital punishment back in 1846, but its citizens were in a different mood these days. Columbine, Virginia Tech, the DC snipers, Gabriele Giffords, *The Dark Night* movie, and Newtown wore them down. Then a new senseless gun massacre at a Grand Rapids elementary school pushed them into vindictiveness. An unbalanced young man with an automatic rifle got into a full school bus and emptied two magazines. It was ended when a teacher kicked open the door and jumped the shooter as he fumbled in his dropped bag for another magazine. The people who aligned to keep guns easily accessible lined up again for executing gun murderers. A constitutional amendment allowing capital punishment passed easily, and the legislature put out a bill setting it up.

The new liberal governor did not veto the capital punishment bill, although she said she was against it. It was passed as part of the budget bill, and she could have used her line-item veto. She was advised that both legislative houses—line-item vetoes could be overturned by a mere simple majority—would have taken it out of her hands and made her look soft.

As a savvy lawyer politico, she was not inclined to grant a reprieve or stay of execution for Frank. It would have been unpopular. His case was open-and-shut, and he wasn't requesting a stay. That made it easier. She might have felt bad about it under other circumstances. The people had spoken—or perhaps grunted, in this case.

Frank's was to be the first death sentence carried out under the new law. His court-appointed lawyer told him there was a possibility of a temporary stay, pushing off the ultimate sanction further, but Frank didn't care.

He had done the crime, and he knew that nothing he could do would convince people otherwise, so he told his lawyer to stop putting off the inevitable. It was easier for him knowing when he was going to die.

Frank's crime started when he provoked a fight in a bar over a shot in a pool game. He claimed someone bumped him. This was contested, and a man knocked Frank down in the ensuing fight. Frank went home and got his gun. By the time Frank returned, the man was leaving, and Frank shot him in the guts in the street. Then Frank taunted him a while as the man moaned and squirmed. "That's what you get when you mess with me," Frank said in his face. Then Frank shot him again in the temple—killed him because he could, and because nobody could treat him that way. Actually, the prosecutor proved Frank started the fight and the man simply defended himself. The murdered man's wife brought their two kids and spoke at the sentencing, but the judge and the jury needed no convincing that the death penalty was the way to go.

In the execution chamber, another white room, there were six small one-way glass witness windows and a gurney. Also, the room was filled with four guards. Frank did not fight when he was secured with six soft-lined leather restraints—head, body, arms and hands, hips, and two for the legs. A doctor and a male nurse connected two saline intravenous lines, one in each arm, and a heart monitor. Frank was covered up to his neck with a sheet.

Two guards left to make way for the chaplain, and

Frank was given the opportunity to pray and make a public statement.

"I don't pray. What does God care?" Then, thinking something more was expected from him, he added, "I'm sorry I killed the guy. Tell the man's family I'm sorry for them." It was easier to say those things than not.

He paused and watched the chaplain, the warden, and the assistants accept his words as natural repentance. This was a little more than Frank could take, so he added, "How about those Red Wings! Aren't they something?" He had a fleeting feeling that he might have spoiled the sentiment of the first remarks, but he didn't care.

Frank's very last utterance was for the outwardly Christian warden. He locked eyes with him and said quietly to his face, "Come on, let's get this late-term abortion over with." The warden winced, and Frank smiled.

After the witnesses were in place, the doctor checked everything. The warden went somewhere—the doctor said he went to the witnesses' room to announce the execution was about to begin. He returned to his position by the gurney in the chamber and took off his glasses, the arranged signal for the chemicals to be released to the injection leads.

According to Amnesty International, the three drugs utilized in lethal injections include sodium pentothal (a sedative intended to put the inmate to sleep), Pavulon (stops breathing and paralyzes the muscular system), and potassium chloride (causes the heart to stop). It is said death by lethal injection is not painful and the inmate goes to sleep prior to the fatal effects of the Pavulon and potassium chloride.

Others contend that the chemicals together burn like hellfire from every nerve ending, but by then the prisoner is unable to communicate.

The warden pronounced Frank dead, and a physician certified that death had occurred. The witnesses were escorted to the elevators, and Frank's body was released to the medical examiner. His execution was front-page news in both the *Free Press* and the *Detroit News*, and it was noted as "Michigan's first execution since statehood, before the Civil War" by Scott Pelley on CBS at six thirty.

Rex Sivle Declines

REX SIVLE DREW A DEEP BREATH. HE WAS ALL SHOOK up. When the executive director phoned him at his downriver office to give him the "good news," Rex's mind flushed with the flattery. But after the call, he started to worry. Hot beads of sweat seeped onto his upper lip and through his hairline. He dreaded the extra attention, but when the staffer who did the agency newsletter called minutes later to ask a few questions, he felt compelled to cooperate. Even then, he was careful of what he said. Tomorrow, they would take his photo. Rex was to be honored as 1997 employee of the year.

It was too much—story and photo in the newsletter and accepting the award at the annual dinner. How many would be at the dinner? Maybe two hundred. He had avoided these dinners for nearly two decades. He had developed panic attacks in crowds. That one time, at the Burger King at the mall, and a couple of other times, he had to leave quickly. Still, the situation was salvageable. Nothing had happened yet, and maybe nothing would happen if he acted now. Potentially, he could lose everything. The contentedness of his reinvented existence would be destroyed, and he might find himself back in the unlivable lifestyle. His soul would not be his own. So he resolved to return this award to its sender.

Rex took several more deep breaths, and his heart slowed. He had escaped his old life. Returning to his old ways would finish him off. For a long time now, Rex could just go to work in the morning and come home when he was done. Not bring it with him. No impossible demands. Never again, the fast lane. He liked doing something that was worthwhile. He was done with the drugs. He no longer checked in at the Heartbreak Hotel, he joked to himself, and mentally, he had learned to deal with isolation and lonesomeness. Rex was something of a recluse. Books, TV, and cooking were his recreation. He had no close friends, but he corresponded with his ex and their daughter, who had recently ended a short and bizarre marriage.

Life's luck and a little talent from when he was young had left Rex as rich as Midas. In early middle age, he had an accident that nearly killed him. He had to change. A twelve-step program and plastic surgery helped. He learned that life can end in an instant, so you must concentrate on the worthwhile. He learned to live modestly

Rex had become a great reader, which he thought was the best revenge on life's vagaries. He had more time for vacations too. He loved Deutschland, mostly Bavaria, and Switzerland. He flew the SST to Frankfort.

Years ago, his "friends and neighbors," the letter said, selected him to do a tour of West Germany. The discipline and routine of the army gave him the best two years of his earlier life. He made buck sergeant. More recently he had studied German and could converse and correspond with European acquaintances.

Almost seventeen years ago, he answered a newspaper ad for a part-time van driver position with a community mental health agency. He had some reliable references, and he was hired. The supervisor was glad to have a good-sized mature man taking the job. Working with the mentally ill wasn't easy. He had to drive his charges to and from their group homes and day programs. Usually he was the lone worker on the van, but his mind was unworried. If a passenger acted out, Rex would pull off the road and wait until the passenger regained control. Rex was big enough to intervene physically, if required. The consumers, as they were called, liked him. He would sing to them sometimes, but only on the country roads and not when he had high-functioning talkative consumers on board. He was very kind, and frequently the program supervisors would find additional duties for him. He soon became a full-time staff person, driving the van and helping the consumers at the treatment program.

Eventually, a correspondence college accepted Rex's high school credits, and he worked for years to complete a bachelor's degree in sociology. He loved studying sociology and psychology—it was therapy. So much more of life was now clear to him. His studies raised his consciousness. After two years of night classes, he got a master's degree in social work. Now, pushing sixty years old, and after all that he had been through, he was going to be a professional social worker, a clinician, having put in his required supervised counseling hours. It was wonderful. He never doubted that he was making a difference in people's lives.

Slowly but surely he built up his courage for the call. *It's now or never*, he thought at his social worker's desk, which was placed against the wall so as not to be a barrier between counselor and consumer. He picked up the telephone to call the big boss man, who only a few hours before had given Rex the news.

"I'm sorry, sir, I would like to say I appreciate you offering me Employee of the Year; that's all right, but I want to decline it."

"Oh no. Tell me why."

"Just because, sir. I mean, after careful evaluation, I just don't think I deserve it. I do my job, as best I can, but so does everyone else."

"No, you do an extra-special job, and we want to recognize you for it. The committee agreed."

"With all due respect, sir, I still want to decline. It's too much. I don't want other people to think I think I'm better than they are."

"People know how hard you work. You deserve the award."

Rex had hoped for a little less conversation. "You don't know me, sir. I don't like special attention. I think awards give people suspicious minds and make them envious. And I think someone with more seniority as a social worker, who wants the award and wants to be singled out, should get it. I just want to be everyone's teddy bear and do a good job. Thank you for the offer, but no thanks, please."

"Okay, if you feel that way. Would you mind keeping the offer under your hat? When we give it to someone else, we don't want them to know they weren't our first choice. They will feel differently about the award than you do."

"You can count on me. I won't blab. Thank you, sir."

"Can't change your mind? You should have it."

"Don't, sir. You're a heartbreaker. Thank you once again, but no."

"Good-bye, then."

"Good-bye, sir. Auf Wiedersehen."

Big One-Hearted Tennis

A DARK-HAIRED MAN AND A BLONDE WOMAN, BOTH tall and dressed in matching blue shorts and white Polo shirts, packed up to leave one of the middle tennis courts in the wooded park. Rick, his partner following, caught the opening fence door and said in exchange, "Good morning" to the couple as they exited.

"Nice having something like tennis to do together," Rick remarked to his partner as he tilted his head toward the couple walking away.

Rick had arranged this match with his old friend, and, arriving at midmorning, they had expected to wait, sitting on the benches on the first nice spring day in Michigan. "This is like having a reservation. Don't you just love it?" He put his tennis bag down and looked the park over. He appreciated tennis as an outdoor game, but he used to play in a winter indoor league at the club. He was annoyed with himself for not playing for many years, and he was reconsidering his priorities. Recently, he had called up a local pro and had two lessons. The Ravenswood Park Courts were the best. Located between two fashionable neighborhoods, they had good nets with center straps and high fences with mesh windbreaks.

He stripped off the plastic lid of the tennis ball can and pulled the sealing tab. *Whoosh.* The rubbery smell of brand-new balls greeted him. Rick poured them into his hand, dropping one. It struck his foot and rolled away. He caught up with it and gave it a bop with his racket. The ball bounced up to his hand.

A robin landed on the court and snatched up a large worm that had crawled in from the grass. Then the bird flew up and over the fence, crossing the sun. Rick followed its shadow down the line of the other courts. His heart lightened as he felt the old feelings. *Can't be down on a day like this.*

From the first warm-up stroke, he was swinging freely. With his semi-Western grip, he hit the sweet spot of his oversize racket. *Swoosh–ping!* The ball sailed over the net to his opponent's baseline with heavy topspin. He jumped up and down several times to get the blood in his legs. He moved forcefully, forward, backward, and laterally. As he closed in on the net for a volley, he rediscovered unused reflexes. He moved toward his opponent's return before it had cleared the net. The trademark on the ball was visible as it swept toward him, and the ball seemed to slow down.

When warm-ups were over, his opponent, an attorney, made an elaborate show of spinning his racket and covering the handle butt logo with his hand. "This is my racket formerly known as Prince," he said with a smile.

Rick laughed. Not all lawyers are blood-sucking divorce shysters. He called "up," and the racket end unveiled was *P* on the butt end, right side up and he won the serve. His practice serves were mostly long, and his first two game serves were also long, a double fault. For the serve on the second point, he spun the ball more and it tucked in. After several baseline exchanges, Rick won the point. Change it up. He came in on the next three first serves and received weak returns, but he muffed two of the next three volleys. *Just nerves, anxiety. Relax.* He was down 30–40 and in jeopardy of losing his service game—the first of the outdoor season. *Don't get down on yourself. Raise your intensity; refocus.* He roughed up the ball knap against his shirt, preparing to serve. He tossed it a little higher in a slight arc toward the net. His legs flexed and straightened; his trunk coiled and then spun forward. His arm struck up and out, and his wrist snapped. The ball shot over the net and clipped down just inside the service line. It whizzed past his opponent, who was so late in preparation that he couldn't manage a decent swing at the ball. *Ace!*

His opponent, a man in similar circumstances, also used to play at the tennis club in the winter. They knew each other's strengths and were evenly matched. As the set progressed, they each gave up one service break, but at five–four, Rick held an advantage. Not giving in, his opponent drew Rick wide with a crosscourt shot after Rick hit a short return to the ad court. Rick had to scramble. From his backhand side, he moved his weight toward the ball and began his swing. But this time he brushed up on the ball harder and put some spin on it. His motion until the very end was identical to his regular backhand shot.

Rick had seen his opponent rush the net. *The guy thinks he can cover any shot down the line or crosscourt because I'm running, making the shot under stress.* Rick watched his perfect topspin lob sweep over the outstretched racket of his opponent and then kiss the baseline. A two-handed-backhand lob made on the run! The set was his.

Rick served to begin the second set, as he had the first. His opponent was gearing up for a comeback, and he was starting to clock Rick's serve. Rick began serving harder and with more topspin and less slice, causing the ball to kick. He was swinging up at the ball, hitting with an almost vertical motion as he struck it with forward force.

Now Rick was up an ad at 40–30. His serve was returned down the line for a passing shot. Rick lunged and struck the ball deep and crosscourt. His opponent seemed to have anticipated this, so he ran the shot down and returned crosscourt. Rick nailed his ball down the line with topspin to win the first game of the second set.

Service was going well, but his opponent was holding up. Both players held service until it was three–three. Then Rick began to serve the seventh game. Two courts down, he noticed two college girls playing. The shorter one was a friend of his daughter. The other one was a tall blonde with quick legs, strong glutes and great lateral movement, like Maria Sharapova. *Poetry in motion sliding along the baseline.* He watched her hit a couple of shots. Rick lost the next three points. *Okay, focus on the action on this court,* he thought to himself.

On the fourth point, the return popped up right in his power zone. Rick smoked it. He watched his racket hit the ball, and the ball vanished instantly across the net. But the sound he heard was *sprong!* He had broken a string. His opponent returned the ball, and Rick tried to hit it back with the tensionless strings, but it fell short into the net. The point and the game were lost. He was broken, now three–four.

No matter. Rick took a breath, smiled, and looked up at the blue sky. Nothing would spoil this day. He walked over to his bag and pulled out his identical spare racket. He drank from his water bottle. *Stay hydrated, stay positive.*

Rick wanted to break back immediately, and soon he was leading love–forty on his opponent's service. The fourth point started a long exchange of deep topspin baseline shots. For ten strokes, they punched and counterpunched like boxers. Then Rick moved, took a ball early, and increased the return angle with a crisp low one. But his adversary ran this one down as well, so Rick, now near the center on the service line, shifted his body over and hit to the opposite side. His opponent had to run a long way and now was totally out of position. Rick received a weak, although deep, shot down the line to his forehand. It was the wrong shot. Rick covered it with a sharp crosscourt forehand to the deuce court. His opponent didn't even try to run it down. A winner! It felt great, and the set was even at four all.

It was Rick's service. For most of the match he had served to his opponent's backhand. *Must change things up.* Rick served a hard slice to the deuce court, forehand sideline. It was a surprise, and it drew a short high return off the rim of the racket. Rick was coming to the net on his serve and quickly closed in on the ball, but the ball cut into him and dropped. Right-handed Rick mentally transposed and executed Rafael Nadal's left-handed slice backhand crosscourt drop volley for an ad court winner. He held serve.

A loud siren broke the almost pastoral silence of the morning. A big chartreuse fire engine blasted its way out of the neighborhood firehouse behind the courts across the street. The sound penetrated though Rick's chest and hurt his ears. His heart skipped a beat, and he stopped playing. *Blatt! Blatt!* The amplitude zapped his nerves again as the diesel engine revved and pulled from the drive into the street. *Nee-naw, nee-naw, nee-naw!* It completed the turn and accelerated away.

Rick walked over and sat on a court bench. He leaned forward and put his head in his hands to stop them from shaking. Then he pulled out a bottle of water from his tennis bag. "Let's take a little break."

His opponent came over and sat down briefly but soon got up and walked back to his court position. "Come on, let's play. There's a fire somewhere. Don't let it break your heart."

"No problem. *Ha!* No argument." Rick got up.

Refocus. Take control.

Now his opponent was serving to stay in the match. *Five–four, shut the door,* Rick said to himself. They hit back and forth, back and forth, baseline to baseline multiple times, and Rick grew impatient. He took a crosscourt shot to his forehand early and hit the ball with all the forward force and topspin he could muster. It was designed to go down the line hard and fast, with the topspin pulling it down just before the line for a winner. Maybe he hit it too hard; it would be either a clean winner or it would be out. But no! It hit the tightly drawn net cord with a loud snap, bounced high, and then dropped down just on the other side of the net short, with no possibility for a return. Rick knew he didn't deserve the point. The ball probably would have been long. Sometimes it's better to be lucky than to be good. He held his racket up in tennis apology. It was love–fifteen.

Rick decided to take a chance and move in on the first serve. He returned hard and sharp to the line, and he closed in on the net. He saw that his opponent was on the run; the return would be weak.

Ah! It's a lob over my head. He scrambled back, running sideways. The lob was high, and he had a chance to run it down. Rick knew one trick shot. He ran and caught up with the ball after it bounced, and it fell over his left side as he faced the back fence. When the ball dropped to a foot from the ground, he swung up behind it, and swatted at it low between his legs. *The Sabatweeni!* The shot went straight and low over the net near the sideline. Rick turned just in time to see it land. His opponent, waiting at the middle of the net, stood dumbfounded. Love–thirty.

The trick shot at this stage of the game seemed to deflate his opponent, and he double-faulted his next serve. Rick waited for a match–point serve. Saving his best for last, his opponent served hard with topspin at Rick's body. It handcuffed him. Still Rick kept his one-handed backhand wrist stiff and pushed the ball deep to his opponent's ad corner. The reply was a short low lob that would not overarch. Rick steadied, switched to his continental grip, and pointed up at the ball. *A short lob is a gift from the gods. Don't mess it up. It's Christmas in springtime.* But it was taking too long. *Oh, hurry up.* He stepped toward the net. *Wait for it! Don't drive it into the net, and don't hit it long. Don't screw it up. You know what to do.* The ball fell down into range, and Rick hammered it into midcourt. It bounced out of play over the fence with no chance for a return.

Rick did the half-version of Jimmy Connors's tight-fisted dance—one pump, one jump, trying not to be a hot dog. Next time, his friend might beat him. Rick shook his friend's hand and said, "Nice playing. Hope we can play a lot more."

His opponent was a good sport but didn't like losing. Rick knew the guy was thinking how he was going to work on the backboard and develop a deeper second serve before playing again.

Rick reflected for a moment and noted that, with the exception of Connors, his tennis idols were twenty years younger than he. No matter. He congratulated himself on still moving well and liking the physical game.

Rick was happier than he had been for a long time as he walked back to his car. He stood on a treated log that was used to mark the parking lot, and a bunch of grasshoppers flew out from underneath. He looked around at the park—people playing, people coming and going. The courts were still full. He would remember this perfect day for a while, although he would play two or three times a week all summer. He didn't feel like going back to his apartment. He wished he had his iPad to read. Rick was glad he had burned so many calories in this two-set match. He decided to go through the drive-through for lunch and maybe pick up Chinese takeout for dinner.

Second Person, Sixty-Seven

RIDING NORTH TO SAN FRANCISCO ON A HALF-EMPTY Greyhound bus, you doze much of the trip. Raindrops smear against the window. From the interstate highway in slate-gray April, the wet road and bare foliage look much like the Midwest. You remark to yourself, not audibly, *You finally got a little break.* Exhale in frustration.

It's been fourteen weeks since you were away from the army in civilian clothes. Eight weeks of basic training in Georgia and then on a plane to advanced infantry training in California—things happen fast in the service. You've gained more than twenty-five pounds, all muscle, in three and a half months. They can't kick sand in your face now. Basic training made you tough—stronger and quicker than you've ever been. As you awaken in the bus seat, you flex and loosen your new shoulder and neck muscles.

How good it is to be away from the goddamn fucking drill sergeants. You hate taking orders from shouting assholes, but you relish the physical stuff. You like running, bayonet training, and hand-to-hand combat. You developed a knack for it. When they sent you to California, you knew orders for Vietnam were inescapable. You got them yesterday. You'll be in-country, as they say, in a month. Will you have what it takes? You have your doubts. Will you choke? Will you chicken out? Can you pull the trigger? Can you actually kill a fellow human being? You fear inadequacy and the responsibility of killing more than the danger of combat.

Most of your friends from high school are already over there or returned home already. They passed the test, made it back—even that dipshit Arnie. Arnie could fuck up a wet dream. He was a joke all the way through school, but he did two tours in 'Nam, mostly fixing radios in Saigon. Not a scratch. If he could do it, you can.

So after fourteen weeks they're giving out passes on account of your whole company getting orders to Vietnam. You embark on a celebratory bus trip to San Francisco. It'd be a shame if Fort Ord, a sandy, rain-soaked shit hole, was the only piece of California you ever saw.

Hours later, on Fisherman's Wharf, you're consecrating the 'Nam orders by eating like a condemned man. You're feasting on surf and turf, a terrible extravagance for a slick-sleeved private, E-2. You couldn't decide on something from California. What is abalone? You sip a glass of the house white with the lobster. The wine tastes like piss. You order a Budweiser.

Looking out the window at the cold, gray bay, it seems like years ago, but it isn't, that you bombed out at —— State University. Things happened. Your life became unglued. What's the point? Lost motivation and concentration, couldn't go to class. Drank too much—as much as you could—stayed up late, slept late. After your last semester, you volunteered for the draft a month before they would have drafted you anyway. Might as well get it over with. The draft board's letter actually said, "Your friends and neighbors have selected you …" Christ! What would distant enemies do to you?

Chug down your beer. This place is too classy for your tastes. Where else to go? You used to play the guitar and sing gentle folk songs. Makes no sense now. Flunked out, drafted, on your way to 'Nam. Can't read anything serious either. No philosophy. Can't Kant. Neither Sartre, nor Camus. Doesn't mix with army bullshit. Head is filled with things like getting both your damn ammo packs on your pistol belt in the morning so the drill sergeant doesn't ream you a new asshole.

"Give me twenty, Private!" he yelled, Smokey Bear hat brim touching your helmet.

"Yes, Sergeant!" you scream as you hit the dirt, counting off push-ups.

It's stopped raining, and it's drying out. Where next? The song says that if you're going to San Francisco, you should "be sure to wear some flowers in your hair." What hair? They shaved it all off the first day. You got special parade duty the last week in basic, and they shaved it all off again. You look like a freak, a real freak, not a longhair. Maybe after the army you'll grow your hair long, so why not visit the flower children? You know where they are.

A city bus drops you off right in the middle of the district, and you haven't been there an hour before you fall in with a bunch of longhairs sitting on the corner. Guys and girls just hanging out. Incense is burning away on the sidewalk. They openly pass a joint around, but the longhairs don't offer you, the skinhead, a hit. You're not into that anyway. All the guys around you could pose for Jesus and the disciples in bell-bottom blue jeans and tie-dyed shirts. You look like a chemotherapy patient. No wonder they don't trust you. Half-drunk, it's hard to reach across the cultural differences between peace freaks and a trained killer. They find out you haven't a place to stay for the night, and one longhair, hugging his girlfriend, offers to put you up at his place. An offer of kindness to impress the girl. He knows you won't take him up on it. You thank him for the offer but say you're not sure what you are going to do, which is true enough.

It's boring just sitting around on the sidewalk, hanging out. Your cold butt hurts from sitting on the cement. Get moving. You find a couple of uniformed sailors in a bar and start palling around with them. They are on pass, too, off a ship, and they are really drunk. The smaller sailor sweeps a beer bottle off the table, and it smashes on the floor. Glass skids fifteen feet over to the bar. Bartender yells at sailors to get the hell out or he'll call the police. Mouthing off to the bartender, the sailors leave. You leave too. You've joined them out of military solidarity.

Three of you are walking down the street, looking for another bar. Man, they are really shitfaced. The smaller, drunker one is still way out of control. He picks up a piece of curbing that's cracked off onto the street. For no reason you know of, he chucks it through a storefront plate glass window. Glass shatters and cascades down on the sidewalk. You cross the street and walk fast up the block to distance yourself from those fucking sailors. Cops arrive almost immediately, but you're out of there.

It's getting dark. You're a little too drunk to be walking around Haight–Ashbury at night. Maybe no one should walk alone at night around here. But this is the first pass off the base you've had, and you want to make the most of it. You walk under an old overhanging marquee of a closed movie house, and a big badass black guy gets in your face and says, "Hey man, give me all your money."

Your mind isn't too clear, but you don't want to give up the little money you have left. Big badass black guys scare the shit out of you, and they also piss you off. You say, "Fuck you, asshole," and turn to walk away.

You realize you should have either given him all your money or run like hell. Perhaps both. Walking wasn't the best option. There's a loud smack on the side of your head. Sounds like a brick dropped on the pavement. He has hit you. It doesn't hurt. Just a jar and a big sound. *Bang!* He's hit you again.

You grab his arm as he tries to hit you some more. You hit him in his ear. The crease between his ear and his head begins to bleed profusely. You hit him again. He ducks down to grab you. He's going to pick you up and crash you to the cement. You push him farther down, and you knee him hard in the face. His nose and mouth begin to bleed. His blood is all over both of you as you struggle on the sidewalk. You tangle legs, and you throw him down. His cheek grinds on the pavement. You watch him start to get up, and you try to walk away again.

He catches up and from a side angle tries to pivot kick you in the nuts. You turn away but still get the full force of the kick on the front of your thigh. It hurts like holy hell. But you've seized his offending foot, and you jack up his foot clear above your head. As he flips over, you smash his head down on the concrete. You're still holding his leg out, so you heel stomp his nuts as hard as you can. You let his leg go, and it falls like a rag doll's. You see his friends coming after you. You run back down the block toward where the police car is still running its overhead lights. You hear his friends curse you and mock you, call you motherfucker. But they don't follow very far.

You look back at the still motionless heap on the sidewalk. You worry you might have killed him, the way he landed. You heard a crack when his head struck the cement. *Did his neck snap?* You decide to go back to the bus station. Stuff your bloody jacket in the trashcan. You can buy another, a different color, at the PX. You take the next bus back to Fort Ord, which looks a little better to you when you arrive. In the barracks, you clean up, take a shower, and sleep it off.

Good morning! Your head hurts inside and out. Your big, new blue-and-purple bruise on your thigh aches for several days. By the weekend, it's nearly gone. You get a pass and board the bus to Monterey. Maybe when you get back from 'Nam, you'll visit San Francisco again and try the abalone.

Elevator Race

Mark looked up from his desk papers to see Pauline, in a red business suit, crossing from the door, carrying what he assumed was the quarterly report. She was attractive and moderately tall.

"Here it is," she said. "Look it over and tell me what you want changed." When she delivered the papers, he noticed her dark hand with lighter palms and nails painted red, matching. It was just a casual observation, her fingers on the pages, more contrast. Mark thanked her and said he doubted it would need many changes.

"Let me know," She turned and walked out the door, heading down to her own office. He put the report aside for a few minutes. There was plenty of time to look at it, and he knew it would be in good shape. He and Pauline had discussed how he wanted the data displayed. He outlined the narrative, and she would take his ideas and run with them. His previous administrative assistant produced reports near the deadline that required too many last-minute changes and sometimes an extension from Lansing.

He hired Pauline with improvements in mind, and he congratulated himself on keeping race out of the hiring equation. With her, he wanted a competent assistant and he didn't want any problems. So he spent a lot of time training her and telling her what he expected. He also encouraged her to ask questions. More than once, Mark reflected on how well this worked out. He also knew Pauline, who was experienced and wanted to succeed, was the main reason it worked out so well.

It had taken Mark a long time to evolve himself to where he was. He felt okay with black people, and usually he was at ease with diversity throughout the building. But you always had to be careful. A white male authority figure could easily offend someone's delicate sensibilities, even in 2000. His office had provided several classes on cultural awareness. *It is best*, he thought, *to stick to business, where there is less chance to be misunderstood*. Friendship or casual horsing around, well, you had to be extra careful there. Just look at all the loose comments by national politicians and celebrities that got them in trouble.

Reactions concerning values, emotions, and sensitivities had to be considered and obviated when possible. Once, years ago, in a sports conversation, he spoke admiringly of George Brett, the Kansas City ball player, who almost hit .400. At that time, Brett was just about the only person to get close to .400 since Ted Williams. So when the black guy he was talking with started spouting the virtues of Rod Carew, Mark was kind of miffed by the change in subject. What the hell did Rod Carew have to do with this conversation? Then he realized that Carew, a black player, was the other guy who had chased .400. When he talked about Carew's abilities—he *was* a Carew fan—the black man began to appreciate the George Brett story. You gotta pay attention.

Mark tried not to be racially naive. How much he had changed in such a short time! Maybe it wasn't such a short time, twenty years or more. But now Mark was a man of the new millennium. Mostly, he just carried on his job without race or culture being an issue. Often he nearly forgot about it completely, and with someone like Pauline, he was a little embarrassed if it even entered his mind. It hadn't always been this way.

Growing up in a small town and returning to work there, Mark had attended a small private college and had developed a one-sided vision of the human race. Other races, especially blacks, were exotic. In his hometown, he lived a Norman Rockwell country existence. He labored for a local enterprise for several years, married, and started a family. It was the nice life he expected to lead. But with the advantages came disadvantages. Often the more interesting movies never played at the local theaters. The culture was pretty limited, and there was little public disagreement. In politics, voters favored the familiar candidates with the least controversy surrounding them.

On the television news, if a story featuring a racial problem came on, he tuned out mentally. He didn't watch television shows that had mostly black casts, because they just didn't appeal to him. One exception was *The Cosby Show*. He felt that Cosby and a few other minorities were mainstream persons and were just like everybody else—ordinary Americans. He would not describe himself as a racist, and racial issues just did not occur to him. He had simply lived his whole life in the company of people pretty much like himself.

In his early thirties, Mark found he needed a master's degree to be considered for promotion. The community college couldn't help him, so he applied by mail to Wayne State University, in the center of Detroit, to take evening classes. Before classes started, he had to drive down to see his advisor, whose office was on the twenty-third floor of an old thirty-story office building.

Taking the afternoon off, he sped down to the city on the interstate. After an hour, as he neared downtown, he shifted and squirmed in this seat. He squinted at the exit sign and worried that he might get it wrong and end up God knows where. He drove off the exit ramp, swinging low in a river of cars, and descended to neighborhood level. The street was lined with old brownstone apartment houses. Instant ghetto!

At a traffic light, he pressed the electric door lock button. The thump was audible to persons on the street; one man sitting on a front porch looked up at him and seemed to take the sound as an affront. What did the guy expect? Mark thought the man looked like the actor-footballer Bernie Casey, though maybe not as tall, or as big, and probably darker.

Detroit hadn't been a part of his life, except for things like the Tigers. He had come down to the ballpark, but that was like an isolated downtown island. At the ballpark, you just parked your car, saw the game, and then returned on the same freeway. A couple of times, he attended a business conference at the Renaissance Center—another island separating guests from city contact. He found the parking structure from the campus map. The early September afternoon was turning hot, and he walked several blocks to the tall, old office building housing his advisor. All kinds of people were on the street bordering the campus— blacks, Asians, Hispanics, and various Middle Eastern people. He didn't know how to interact. Should he look at them or away? He hurried into his advisor's office building and walked over to the elevators. From the directory, he confirmed that his advisor's department office was on the twenty-third floor.

The elevator doors opened, and people rushed through. All the faces and heads he could see before him were black. There were men bigger than he was; one was tall enough to be a basketball player. The thought of getting on the elevator made his upper lip sweat. His heart beat faster, and his anxiety amplified. There's always room for one more. A semicircle of space hollowed out for him, placing him near the middle of the front.

An eclectic collection. He could see that. Men and women in business suits, a man in a dark green maintenance uniform, and office workers. There were at least three women. One in the back, whose face he couldn't see, wore a business suit coat and skirt, and one stocky woman wearing big eyeglasses and a dress stood in front. The third was young and pretty, maybe a student. He stepped to enter the elevator, balked, and then stepped again. Some of them seemed to notice his hesitation.

Inside he leaned over and pressed 23. He turned back forward and read "Otis" on the threshold of the car as the doors closed over it. Getting warm, he flapped his sport coat for air. He needed more air to breathe as well. As his eyes adjusted to the dimness in the elevator, he told himself that this was a random selection of persons. *They don't even know each other. They won't bite. They're not paying you any attention. You're the one who has boxed this in as a racial situation. You're just confined in a small space with a bunch of ordinary people.*

The elevator didn't move. Was it stuck? What would he do trapped in an elevator with all of these black people? How long would it be? Could he get enough air? The car's delay in starting seemed like forever, but no one else noticed. Somewhere, steel cables, cinched by wheels, began to hoist with a stuttered jerk.

No one broke the closed-in code of silence. There were elevator noises: cables, pulleys, winches, humming, doors opening and closing, voices of people on the floors as the elevator passed on up. Most passengers avoided eye contact, looking at the ceiling and the floor or watching the floor numbers change. The elevator stopped on the third floor, and two men got off. One got on, a black man. Mark felt his knees and ankles compress as the car started again. It stopped next on the ninth floor. He thought the hazel-eyed man who was getting on was white, but then he realized the man was black, though light-skinned.

The elevator jumped and then stopped between floors. Behind him, a man quietly said, "Damn," and it seemed they all nodded or shifted in some way. It was as if it were a rehearsed signal. Previously Mark had noticed no elevator Muzak, but now he began to hear jungle noises, birds calling, creatures screeching, and then drums being beaten. This segued into what he thought were Motown-ish sounds. "I feel good," James Brown announced from the hidden speaker. The elevator began to move.

Mark was dizzy, hot, claustrophobic, and about to swoon. Everything was happening at once. His balance wavered, and big, strong hands—black hands—grabbed his arms and held him fast. The younger woman reached inside his coat, unbuttoned his shirt, and began to rub his chest. She kissed his neck and breathed huskily in his ear. She pressed her breasts against his arm. The stocky woman began to fumble with the zipper of his pants. He was too startled to scream when another hand reached out in front of his face and thumbed a hypodermic needle, squirting clear liquid. The tall man reached over his head and snapped open a shiny, straight-edged razor, and he started to rub the dull side against Mark's cheek. Raucous rap music filled his ears as he neared blackout. The big black man announced, "We gonna cut you, sucka, " following up with a deep voodoo-zombie laugh that was aborted with a jolt.

The music ended, and the elevator stopped, giving Mark a lift inside his shoes. The doors opened to an empty hallway, flooding the elevator car with light. Mark could see "23" ornately engraved on the wall across from the door. He saw "23" lit up on the button panel. Well-worn "Otis" shined up at him.

"Excuse me," said the pretty black woman, stepping around him and walking down the hall. She held a purse, several books, and a spiral notebook. People shifted behind him, and he was gently bumped as he stepped into the hall also.

"Sorry, pardon me," someone said.

Mark turned to look at the people on the elevator. He saw no one acknowledged him. They all looked the same as when he started—looking up, down, or away, saying nothing. Then the man in the dark green uniform, who had been on his right, nodded toward him. Mike Johnson was the name on his university ID badge. The stocky woman held a big purse and a paper lunch bag. The tall man, not so big anymore, was in a coat and tie, dressed as neat as a pin. Mark saw that the man carried a worn, brown satchel-type briefcase. With dark-framed glasses, he looked intelligent, tired, and late-middle-aged. The man with hazel eyes shook his head and rubbed his neck. He appeared to be very much the same as Mark in age, build, and attire. The stocky woman glanced at Mark, then to the button panel. She moved to press the button that would close the doors, but the doors were already closing.

Mark turned around in his new environment, a brightly-lit, white-painted, white-tiled hallway. Having ascended to the floor of his graduate advisor, he was still in his coat and tie, ready for business. He heard the elevator cables rattle as the car continued up to higher floors. The fluorescent ceiling lights buzzed. He reviewed his reflection in the glass covering the floor directory. He straightened his tie and then, like a batter stepping up to the plate, dropped his right hand to make a cursory check of his genitals. He shook his shoulders, took several deep breaths, and walked over to the porcelain drinking fountain. Mark drank and put his face in the stream of lukewarm water.

Brother Cozumel

Just walking from the taxi to the rental car office got me sweating. Away from the sea, there was no wind, and it had to be ninety degrees. I was beginning to wish I had stayed at our Cozumel island resort. A front-window air conditioner, jutting out, chugged away as I went in.

"*Bienvenido*, amigo. Welcome. How may I help you? My name is Humberto."

It sounded like "Umberto," but below his white-toothed smile that made you glad you came in, he had a name badge pinned to his light blue work shirt. After starting the paperwork, he and I went back outside and made the round-car inspection, agreeing on any previous damage there might be. He noted two small scratches on the right front fender of the little red Korean hatchback and marked them on the rental sheet. Then he motioned with his clipboard.

"Let us go back to my office, *mi* amigo, where it is cool."

He returned to his side of a counter that had patches

of wood showing through the worn, gray painted surface.

"You did well to reserve by phone, senor. We kept this excellent performer back for you. It's our last car until tomorrow, when we have some returning." He smiled at me as he reached over the counter, gave me the keys, and shook my hand. His Mayan face, like many Mayan faces, seemed to have a touch of Italian mixed in. He was bigger than average, perhaps five feet eight inches tall and 160 pounds.

"You will have a quality experience with the car."

"Yes, I'm sure I will. Your English is very good. Where did you learn it?"

"I worked for nine years in San Diego, but I had to return. I was illegal. Now it is difficult to go back. I have a job, and I have resettled. I don't make too much money, but it's a living." He shrugged. We conversed briefly more, and then I think he sensed I wanted to go.

"*Bien viaje*. I look forward to your return, amigo." He saluted casually.

"Gracias. Hasta luego." I nodded and waved as I backed through the door into the sunny heat.

Through the week, my wife, Julie, and I used the car only a few times—driving into town or out to dinner. Mostly I just chilled at the Coral Princess, reading under a *palapa*, swimming in the sea, and drinking *cerveza* with chips and *pico de gallo*. We saved the road trip for Thursday.

I braked to make a tight turn to head east out of San

Miguel de Cozumel toward the island's uninhabited eastern coast that faces the Caribbean. Coming straight out of the curve, I pulled the floor shifter down toward me and gunned the gas. The car shot us forward. Its low center of gravity and the tight steering were like those of a sports car. Running through the manual gears, I felt connected to the road, not so insulated as in my SUV with an automatic transmission back in Minnesota. Small is better in the Yucatan, where roads are narrow and gas is expensive.

We stopped at the last stoplight before the long, straight trans-island highway.

"Buddy, shift with me."

"Okay, but I can't shift that fast." Julie scooted toward the center. "We haven't done *this* for a long time." We had an economy stick shift in our first years of marriage.

I revved up the engine and pulled out in first. I pushed in the clutch, and she grabbed the shifter knob with her left hand and pushed it up into second. Similarly, we did third, fourth, and fifth in a partnership that had lasted twenty-six years and counting.

Driving to the beaches that face Cuba's underside was our planned adventure. We knew the route because we had done it in previous years. There was much to do and see. Along with the beach bars and an ATV track, there was a state park. No one stays overnight on the east side, except at one small solar-powered hotel, Ventanas al Mar—"windows to the sea." We always said we would stay at this isolated place. *Next year.* It would be surreal on the dark ocean beach at night, but we preferred the settled west side of the island, where there was more action.

Traversing the island on the narrow highway, the car filled with wind and light when we opened the sunroof and the four windows. The car radio received two Mexican stations, but Julie's Spanish wasn't that good and mine wasn't quite fast enough for radio listening, so the radio stayed off. The speed limit was eighty, which at first glance seemed awfully fast, until I realized, once again, it was in klicks and the equivalent of forty-eight miles per hour. As per the season, the sky was cloudless and had been for the five days we had been here. The road was dry and dusty. If you got behind another car, you had to close your windows and turn on the AC, but traffic was sparse.

We drove right past the turnoff to San Gervasio, the major Mayan ruins site on the island. Apparently it was some sort of pre-Columbian pan-Mayan women's resort, where ladies from all over Maya-land became fertile, or gave thanks for having been fertile, by making sacrifices to Ix Chel, deity of not only fertility but also the moon, childbirth, medicine, and weaving.

"I was as fertile as I wanted to be." Julie said as we passed the sign. "I got two great kids. Two and out. Thanks, Ix Chel."

Driving along, I smiled and bobbed my head. "Yeah, right. Absolutely. But don't be sacrilegious." It was a joke, but Julie frowned. She liked the ruins, but she was not as keen on the Maya as I was.

Coming out to the end of the east–west road, the sea vista opened as a broad panorama pocked by low Mexican beach buildings—a bar and three knickknack shops. A big Mexican flag fluttered above the bar—red, white, and green—accenting the clear blue sky, the darker blue ocean, and the white waves sliding up on a fine sand beach. Loud mariachi music greeted us as we made the turn, and two young men motioned for us to park at the shops. We waved back and drove on, making the turn south. Our destination was Chen Rio, a more intimate place, a bodega-less bar with a clearer view and a better swimming area.

There were cars and mopeds filling the few slots right at Chen Rio. I drove farther down, forty yards or so, and made a U-turn to park where there was a short path down to the beach. The beach was just as good there, and we would be away from bar people and most of the beachgoers.

We had rock shoes and walked over the hot sand and down the path to the beach without problems. After we spread out our towels, we ambled down along the sea edge to the Chen Rio bar, me carrying my daypack with valuables, Julie carrying her beach bag. We sat in plastic chairs at a plastic table under an umbrella and ordered two Sols, a local favorite beer in a clear bottle. Lime wedges were stuffed in the tops.

We asked the waiter to watch our stuff, and we went for a swim. Part of the area near the bar was protected by a natural reef and rock outcroppings that blocked the waves. The ocean was clean, warm, and clear. I wore swimmer's goggles to protect my contacts and keep them from coming out in the water. Through them I could watch small fish near the bottom, working the sand. We floated, buoyed up extra in the salt water. Julie came to me and wrapped her legs around me, and we kissed and kissed again.

"If we stayed at Ventanas al Mar, we could continue under the stars."

"Too spooky. What if a big shark came in." She unclasped me.

There were other swimmers in the water and people at tables near the beach bar. Returning to the bar, we looked at the menu. Pretty limited—fried fish and chicken, various tacos, pico de gallo and chips, beer, and margaritas. We had had early lunch in Cozumel, brought snacks, and planned to have a late dinner in the new restaurant on the second floor of the Museo de la Isla de Cozumel. So I left a good tip and we took our beers.

Back at our beach towels, we set up for an hour or two in the sun. I rubbed her back with high-SPF lotion, and she reciprocated. Before long, our two beers were too warm. I poured my last couple ounces into the sand and tossed the lime wedge out to a nosey seagull. The gull picked it up and shook off the sand. You could tell it wasn't too pleased with the sour lime, but it flew off with it anyway before another gull could steal it. In a while, I went back and got us new Sols.

When I had settled again, I unzipped my daypack. Along with a bottle of water, I had brought three books and the current *New Yorker,* providing some choices for whatever mood I was in. I picked Hemingway's *The Old Man and the Sea,* since I was facing Cuba some one hundred miles or so to the northeast. Looking out to sea, I could imagine the old man with the huge fish lashed to his boat, beating away the scavenging sharks with an oar.

We sat under some palms about fifty feet from the water. There was a rise and a foliage area between the road and the beach. It was fairly distant from all the other parties. We liked to relax and read. There were perhaps forty other bathers stretched out along the beach, which ran about a quarter mile south, away from the beach bar. Our limited privacy didn't last long.

A big, blond Viking-looking guy with a Fu Manchu mustache, swinging a big cooler, was bearing down on us from the beach bar. He was followed by a thin, shorter brown-haired man and two zaftig girls. The three followers carried a bunch of accoutrements— beach bags, blankets, towels, big umbrellas, neck pillows, and magazines. You could see through the girls' rather revealing mesh skirts that they wore thong bikinis. From back at the bar, most of the waiters and the male patrons watched the girls' progress. The group set up camp about twenty feet from us, right in front of the path back to the road entrance. Our new neighbors were laughing it up pretty good, apparently having started early. Their CD player put out an electronic American headbanger beat, but wind whipped most of the sound away.

Not great drinkers, Julie and I were nursing our second Sols. Although I think it would have taken a lot to get pulled over by the police, the idea of spending a night in a Mexican jail for drunk driving didn't appeal to me. We sat there wondering if we should leave.

"Hey, bro, you got an opener? I ripped up my fingers. These Mexican beers aren't twist-off."

Turns out, in my daypack, I had small aluminum opener that I had picked up somewhere. "Here." I tossed it over. "Keep it. I don't need it."

"Much appreciated, *ah-mee-go*," the Viking said. Then he laughed at either his good fortune or his clever use of Spanish.

He opened four beers, "Hey, you want one?"

"No, I got one already. Thanks." After that the wind increased. I was able to ignore them for a while, looking at the water or reading *The Old Man and the Sea*.

The wind blew steadily from the ocean, but it weakened a bit and land scents wafted around—jasmine flowers, road tar and gasoline, and—

"Do you smell what I smell?" Julie said.

"Now that you mention it." She was so good at sniffing out weed that she ought to have worked for the police. I had to peek. The Viking, his buddy, and the two wild girlfriends were passing around a lumpy cigarette, keeping it palmed in their hand or low to the beach towel. I doubt even *la policia*, who patrolled the beach road, would have cared. Maybe the bar staff would complain.

"How come he didn't offer us any of that?"

Julie frowned, looked over at them, and then went back to her book. A few minutes later, I glanced over again, and I couldn't look away. The Viking's girl untied her bikini top from behind her neck, and two spectacular boobs plopped out. The other girl started untying her top, and I found the willpower to return to my book. There were other tops off far down the beach, a long way from the bar crowd, but letting them hang out so close to the bar was kind of pushing it. The Viking's girl had movie-star knockers—enhanced, but spectacular just the same.

I didn't want to gawk, and I was with my wife. But I couldn't keep from taking a quick glimpse once in a while, hoping my sunglasses would cover me. (They say a woman can always tell when you are looking at her breasts or when you are looking at another woman's breasts. Probably they just assume, and they are too often right.)

"I'm hot. Let's go for another dip." Julie said. We walked back toward the bar's reef-sheltered swimming area. The water was warm, but after twenty minutes of puttering around in it, it was still chilling. We sat in the sun and warmed ourselves at the sea's edge; the waves, made small from the protective reef, lapped at our feet.

"Time to move on, eh?"

"Naw, the scenery is great here." *Let's joke about it.*

"Too good. I don't want you to strain your eyes."

"I only checked them out a couple times." I smiled sheepishly.

"So far." She looked at me in mock accusation. "Let me rephrase. Time to move on."

"Okay. No problem." Actually, it was uncomfortable having great knockers hanging about and not being able to admire them. We went back to our beach spot and packed up.

There was only one way back to the car, unless we wanted to walk down to the bar and up to the road from there, backtracking over the gravel and hot pavement. Julie just tromped right behind their blankets and up the path. The girls grabbed towels to cover themselves. I followed along, acting oblivious, carrying my daypack.

My big blonde friend looked up at me like "What are you doing here?" *Screw him.* His group had camped in front of the path, and it was his babes who were showing off to everybody. *He's got a lot of nerve taking offense when somebody looks. What a joke.* I shrugged and tried to convey "Sorry, I couldn't help it. What did you expect?"

By this time, the Viking had put on a light camel-colored hoodie to keep sun off his Nordic skin. With his sunglasses he looked like the Unabomber.

"Take it easy, bro. Thanks for the opener," he said as I passed. I suppose he had decided to be friendly; I couldn't read his face. He held up his fist to chuck, and I chucked it.

"*No problemo.*" And I was up the path.

The next beach bar was more relaxing but less interesting. Julie and I snoozed in shaded, brightly colored Mayan hammocks that swung in the sea breeze.

We swam again and had another Sol. Still not a cloud, and the waves rolled on the beach every few seconds. We read some more. Julie took a photo of me expanding my chest near the sign that said "Topless Photos Only."

We had a great time in Cozumel. Besides our eastside adventure, we had an afternoon of scuba diving, snorkeling behind our hotel, dancing and shopping in town, reading by the pool and the ocean, happy hours with margaritas, and el Museo de la Isla de Cozumel. Now, like part of closing ceremonies, I had to return the car on our penultimate day.

It was still hotter in town, and the air conditioner was still chugging along as I went in the shop.

"*Hola*, Senor Arnold," Humberto greeted me across his worn countertop. "Did you have a quality experience with the car?" We started up like old friends, but another customer interrupted us.

"Hey, man. I got to settle up. Got a ship leaving in half an hour. Let's do it."

It was the fucking Viking, no less. He leaned in at the counter, blocking me off.

"Let's settle up. I got the car at the end of Thirty-Fifth Avenue. It's out of gas. Here's the keys—I gotta go. I'll pay you for the tank fill-up. What do I owe you? Come on, I gotta go. Ship's departing. Come on." He was pushing a fifty-dollar bill at Humberto.

"In a moment. First I have to take care of this gentleman." Humberto pointed at me.

He went out to look at my car, leaving me with

the Viking. I wanted to go over the car with him, but he slipped out too fast. Probably he didn't want the Viking left alone in his office. I could go out and contest any damage that was claimed, but I was sure there wasn't any.

The Viking had a good story, but I wouldn't have believed it. I knew, as sure as the sun rises on the Caribbean, that the car had been bashed up against a building or a tree somewhere on the island, maybe on Avenida 35, *Sur* or *Norte*.

The Viking turned around and considered me for the first time. He thought for a second, and then made out like he had found a long lost friend. Any animosity about my brief ogling of his girl seemed to have been left at Chen Rio.

"I remember you. Good to see ya again." He patted me on the arm and offered his hand, and I shook it.

"Thanks for the opener." he continued. "We wore it out. You guys should have stayed and partied with us." He turned around and leaned backward, putting both elbows on the counter behind him. "What did you think of my babe? Nice tits, huh?" He puffed out his chest, looked at me, and laughed.

"Yeah, she's a looker, all right." I didn't know where to go with this; she did have nice ones.

"Say, bro, you gotta help me with this *chulupa*. I hafta make a ship. Tell him to ring me up ahead of you so I can get on board, okay?" He seemed to consider our last meeting as a great success, and he appealed to me as a fellow American and admirer of the female form.

Humberto came in and said his assistant would be in with my paperwork in a minute.

"Come on. I gotta get moving."

"Where is your car again?" Humberto was a mature man, dark hair graying at his temples. He looked as if he had heard it all before. He was holding out, being obtuse, repeating the same questions, waiting for different answers. "Why isn't the car here?" Probably his tactic was to just keep the guy talking until he told the truth. He had the ace in the hole, a signed copy of the Viking's damage deposit credit card impression, on which Humberto could make any claim. The Viking wanted that back.

The assistant came in with my paperwork and handed it to Humberto.

"It's all *bien*, senor." Humberto gave me my credit card impression for the damage deposit.

"*Hasta la vista*, amigo. I'll see you next time." I should have left it at that. I moved to the door and turned back. "*Él miente*," I added positively as a farewell while I put my hand up to my brow and gave a casual parting salute. I glanced at the Viking, who was watching Humberto. I hoped my Spanish was close enough.

"Gracias. Sí, claro es mentiroso." Humberto nodded. "Cuídate mucho, amigo." He resumed with the Viking. "Why haven't you brought the car in, sir?"

At the airport the next day, Julie and I were shopping at the duty-free Cinco Soles store, getting rid of our last pesos, waiting to board. I bought a T-shirt bearing a big iguana that had a long, skinny, curved tail, and Julie bought a silver bracelet with a tiny sea turtle on it. The sky got darker, and all at once rain drummed and pounded the building. The smell of jasmine and tropical dampness filled the air.

"Are we going to get stuck here?" My first thought was that the flight would be delayed, but after a minute or two, the rain stopped as quickly as it started. Julie came out of the shop, and we took seats in the waiting area near the gate. This was a good time to go to the bathroom before we got on the plane.

"I'm going to the john." I stuffed the Cinco Soles bag with the T-shirt in my carry-on.

"The restroom. Hurry up, I think we'll be boarding soon."

The john was empty when I went in, but after I started doing my business, a man bumped me shoulder-to-shoulder hard enough to make me move my feet.

"You're pissin' in my stall, bro."

What the hell? It was the damn Viking. I felt at disadvantage. Getting angry, I cut short and zipped up. The blonde SOB looked bigger in the confined space, and the edges of his mustache picked up in a confrontational smile. But he seemed unsteady on his feet, so I thought he might just be making a drunken joke, albeit a bad one.

"Very clever, *ah-mee-go*." He made a wide gesture with his right arm, and then he pointed and shook his finger at me, but I was distracted by his colorful arm tattoo with Chinese characters. "Él miente—he lies!

Destiny looked it up in the Spanish dictionary at the resort."

"Destiny? Really? I thought your ship was leaving yesterday. Did you miss it?" I was worried and angry both at the same time. Fight-flight reflexes coming to the fore, I tried not to show the fear, accosted in a restroom. I wished other men would come in.

"If I missed it, it would be thanks to you. No, I never had a ship, just the plane today. I had to pay six hundred dollars for the fender damage. I ought to kick your ass, Senor Él miente."

"Fuck you." This was my all-purpose statement for such situations. I moved to go around him.

"You can't leave; I'm not done with you!"

He swung at me with a left hook, and although I slipped it partially, he caught me in the right side of the head. I grabbed him, pushed him back, and twisted us around so I could break for the door. He pushed me hard, but being shorter, I had leverage. I stepped on his foot and shoved up and away as hard as I could. With one leg held fast and a boozy brain, he couldn't catch himself. He crashed flat-out backward, his head hitting the floor, and he skidded into the wall between the urinals. He began moaning and pulled himself up to a sitting position.

I started for the door, afraid of any involvement with airport security or Mexican police, but I wanted the last word. "No more problems or I'll have la policia on you." I tried to sound tough.

"Eat shit," he said from the floor. He retched once

and spit in my direction. "Kiss my ass." He thrust up his middle finger.

Still angry and full of adrenaline, I turned with the thought of kicking him until he gave up the attitude, but I thought again. I pivoted around, mentally pulled the floor shifter down toward me, gunned the gas, and shot myself out of there. *Keep going.* He was starting to get up.

Two other men passed me coming in as I exited, and I felt fortunate to escape this scene in the foreign airport. Strangely worried that I hadn't washed up, I wiped my hands on my pants.

When I returned to the waiting area, our plane was boarding. We were called in the group after first class. Waiting in line with my boarding pass, I turned to see if anyone was watching us. The Viking and Destiny (looking well tanned in a tight tank top) both glared at me from over near the front of Cinco Soles, their two friends looking into the shop window. In some other venue, the Viking might have had a gun, I suppose. I gave him my squinty Clint Eastwood look with a pained smile. If I ever met him again when he was sober, he would be a different customer. Could he check the flight for our names? It went to Chicago, but we had a transfer to Minneapolis. The plane was full of couples; he couldn't figure out our name without the help of the FBI. If he wasn't leaving on a plane, he might try the Cozumel car rental shop, but I doubt Humberto would cooperate.

In Chicago, Julie looked at me square-on and noticed a slight swelling on the right side of my head.

"What happed here?" She turned my head with her hand and examined it closely.

I smiled awkwardly. "Some guy hit me in the john at the Cozumel airport."

"Yeah, right." she said. "The restroom door probably swung out and hit you."

I thought just a bit. "The jerk hit it real hard, and I couldn't get out of the way."

"Some people. You have to be more careful and watch out for yourself," she said with concern.

"Yeah, that's for sure. Absolutely."

Everyone Hates Malvolio

"HE HATH BEEN MOST NOTORIOUSLY ABUSED," THE beautiful Countess Olivia acknowledged to everyone as I left the grounds with my head bowed, red faced and exhausted. *Why does everyone hate poor Malvolio? I am as fair and constant a fellow as you will find in Illyria.*

"Pursue him and entreat him to a peace," Duke Orsino told two followers, who made after me. Orsino has been my benefactor, but the great man also wanted something from me, and turning to the gathering, he expounded. "He hath not told us of the captain yet."

I don't know how I found my way back to my apartments. I was crushed, betrayed, and angry. Yes, I have been most notoriously tricked this Twelfth Night of Christmas. Gulled by one of the most infamous pranks ever played upon an honest manager, and when all was finished, there was none to tell me why.

I, Malvolio, am steward to the countess and overseer of her magnificent estate and lands. I collect rents from houses and farms and keep accounts. Ultimately, I'm responsible for household concerns, including the servants.

Now that we have discovered the grounds and the authors of this conspiracy, my lady, the Countess Olivia, has assured me, "Thou shalt be both the plaintiff and the judge of thine own cause." I'll be revenged on the whole pack of conniving plotters.

Although I was not born to greatness, to be sure, I have achieved some esteem as the humble servant of the Almighty and my Lady Olivia. I have always strived to be of the greatest benefit and efficacy. People call me puritan for I work hard and expect the same of others. Perhaps there are places where hard work and modest habits are more valued. Here in Illyria, few work unless required, and there is little design to require them. Those of higher birth or station find work distasteful, and they seldom vex themselves in efforts of the mind. Few even of the nobility have bothered to learn reading, and those who can read peruse only commerce and gossip, neglecting learning, science, and the arts.

Time-pleaser also am I called—as if keeping a daily schedule with duties and outcomes expected by the hour, day, week, month, and year were a sin. It is a rough concept at best for my lady's followers. Even the more industrious keep time in their own fashion, and many feel responsibilities should not rule their day. In this household, I alone strive for excellence. I know the rules, laws, and expectations by book and recite them when necessary.

This tale began for me with the arrival, on my lady's estate, of the curious captain of Duke Orsino's inquiry. The captain is a native of a district not three hours from here, where another dialect is spoken and loyalties are doubtful. There are many such divisions in this Balkan region of Illyria on the Adriatic Sea. The captain was stopped on my lady's toll road. In his baggage, he had much material he claimed was salvaged from the sea. This included a set of gentlewoman's garments, about which he would offer no explanation.

"If my tongue blabs, then let my eyes not see," the captain said defiantly at the jail.

Now what could be made of this? A secretive sailor, carrying possibly stolen goods and a mysterious set of gentlewoman's garments, bears watching and requires more explanation. I asked, "What end has come to the privileged owner of these fine clothes?"

So the captain was held in durance on my suit. The sheriff said to this possible pirate, "Tell us more of your cargo, and a sufficient explanation will set your homecoming." For more than two months, the confined captain has kept his secrets.

In this land of Illyria, Duke Orsino rules. We have learned that our arrested captain, having some interest earlier in Orsino's court, presented a young man, Cesario. It is said that the duke was wonderfully pleased with the speech and graceful deportment of this comely youth, and he made him one of his pages. Further, the duke saw special purpose in Cesario and soon treated him with great favor.

Until one year ago, my Lady Olivia's father did I serve. At that time, he took to bed and died. His son, not ready for governing and not well himself, shortly also died. My lady, though healthy, had little preparation to head the manor. I am the only continuity on these lands. By my hand, all is as it should be. The estates of my lady have prospered even while the highest helm has been neglected.

My lady's followers, however, resent my assumed authority and my near complete reign. It has not been easy getting satisfactory work in these times. Of the greatest enviers of my place I name Mariah, chambermaid to my lady; Feste, the court jester; and Fabian, the aspiring laborer. By favors and truculence, Mariah and the rest have recruited two dinner-sucking, noble guests to their cause. These are Sir Toby, my lady's uncle, and his foolish friend, Sir Andrew, a self-supposed suitor to my lady. They are idle and shallow things.

For some time, Feste, the fool, had been absent without leave. I noted as much to my lady, but while she mourned her father and brother, she would not consider punishing the clown. She, of course, held the fool too familiar, and he took advantage. On the day of his return, my lady and I had met in the hallway, and we began discussing the affairs of the estate as we entered her receiving room. The room, like much of the castle, was candlelit, curtains drawn, still in mourning. There was Feste, waiting for her near the hearth of the fireplace. In this season of grief, the clown has been neither required nor greatly missed. The old fool approached in feigned timorousness. He knew the countess would forgive him. As wee ones, he bore her and her brother upon his silly back a thousand times. She would not banish him and suffer another personal loss.

Feste approached her and knelt, saying, "God bless thee, lady!" Mariah, the chambermaid, followed behind him, apparently in some support.

My lady commanded, "Take the fool away." She would have him in the dark cell of the estate reserved for madmen and arrests, awaiting the cart ride to the sheriff's jail.

To my lady's astonishment, Feste told her followers, "Do you not hear, fellows? Take away the lady." Then, stunning all ears, he launched into two convoluted syllogisms implying that my lady was the fool.

Patiently, Olivia again told her followers to take away the fool. To this, with continued gall the clown replied, "Misprision in the highest degree!" Then he launched another tangled argument, parroting Latin phrases, to the effect that my lady was a fool for mourning her brother's soul in heaven. I saw this old jester's joke coming down the Appian Way, but the countess fell for it. My face portrayed my annoyance, so she turned not on him but on me.

"What think you of this fool, Malvolio? Doth he not mend?" I was forced to join in this clever banter. I found it tiresome to jest with a truant fool when there was so much serious business about. And during a mourning period, too!

"Yes, he mends," I said, meaning that at least the old clown had returned. I added that he should be a good fool "till the pangs of death shake him. Infirmity, that decays the wise, doth ever make the better fool." I thought I put him in his place, but the jester was not easily beaten.

"God send you, sir, a speedy infirmity, for the better increasing your folly!" Feste retorted.

"How say you to that, Malvolio?" My lady said, enjoying our debate. This was all I could stand.

"I marvel your ladyship takes delight in such a barren rascal. I saw him put down the other day by an ordinary fool who had no more brains than a stone. Look you now, he's out of his range already. Unless you laugh and minister occasion to him, he is gagged. I protest. I take these wise men, who crow so at these set kind of fools, as no better than the fools' zanies."

Although my words bested the fool, they were not as well chosen as I thought, because my lady took them as a reproach.

"Oh, you are sick of self-love, Malvolio, and taste with a distempered appetite. To be generous, guiltless, and of free disposition is to take those things for birdshot that you deem cannonballs. There is no slander in an allowed fool."

With that, she *allowed* Feste back into the household with no consequences.

Life is never predictable. We have spoken of the curious captain's arrival, washed up with others from a shipwreck some three months earlier. Among the survivors were twins the Adriatic tempest tossed separately, one—whom we know as Cesario—with the captain. The other, Sebastian—presumed drowned—reached the shore elsewhere, saved by a friend. Eventually this preserving tide washed clear to my lady's estates, in the form not only of the captain but also of Cesario.

Sir Toby, drowning with drink as usual, was the first to meet him at the gate. My lady sent me afterward to make a proper response because Cesario was an emissary from the duke. Consumed with love, Orsino was fixed upon on my lady, who would have none of him. So the duke had assigned Cesario, the cleverest and fair young gentleman, to bring his courting.

I must say that my start with the youth was uneven. I told him the countess would not see him, but he would not leave. He had elocution and bearing of a learned gentleman. My lady had instructed me to make excuses as to why she could not see him, but he was fortified against my every denial.

"I'll stand at her doorstep like a sheriff's post and be a supporter to a bench until I speak with her," Cesario told me. He was of medium height for a man, and he had the voice of a high tenor.

In exasperation, I explained to my lady that the young man must be seen. Actually, this audience was not so difficult to obtain. My lady and her gentlewoman have sport with Orsino's handsome pages. In mild interest, she asked his personage and years.

"Not yet old enough for a man, nor young enough for a boy," I told her. "'Tis with him standing in the stream, between boy and man. He is very well favored, and he speaks very shrewishly; one would think his mother's milk were scarcely out of him."

While wooing my lady for the duke, speaking of her favors and of the depth of the duke's love, Cesario courted so remarkably fair that he crossed his purpose. My lady, Countess Olivia, apparently fell head over heels in love with him in short order. *How quickly can one catch the plague!* One must raise an eyebrow at the indeterminate appetite of Olivia—to fall so quickly for this fair but (we now know) counterfeiting youth. Perhaps her love was seeking refuge from the advances of Orsino and Sir Andrew.

My lady once again refused Orsino's suit and sent Cesario away. But she bade the youth come again to say how the duke had taken it. She must have feared she had sent Cesario off for good, that he would not return. So she sent me after him to "give back" an unborrowed ring to him—a ruse to make Cesario return. I did not yet know there was a game afoot. In the street, but several blocks down, I caught up with the youthful rogue.

"Were not you even now with the Countess Olivia?"

"Even now, sir; on a moderate pace, I have since arrived but hither." *An impertinent response to an elder.* I think now Cesario may have been the boldest and the cleverest person in Illyria.

"She returns this ring to you, sir. You might have saved me my pains to have taken it away yourself. She adds, moreover, that you should put your lord into a desperate assurance she will none of him. And one thing more, that you be never so hardy to come again in his affairs, unless it be to report your lord's taking of this. Receive it so."

"She took the ring of me? I'll none of it." He withheld his hand.

"Come, sir, you peevishly threw it to her; and her will is it should be so returned, if it be worth stooping for." I cast it at his feet. "There it lies in your eye; if not, be it his who finds it."

I turned on my heels and left without looking back.

The house routines resumed. By nightfall, Sir Toby and Sir Andrew had awaked from their previous evening's festivities and again had joined reveries in the town. Long after midnight, they came stumbling back to our quiet household, still carousing.

From my chambers, I heard the two come crashing in, opening doors, upsetting furniture, singing, and demanding more food and drink. My lady called me to her chamber and addressed me informally in her robe. She said I should prevail on Sir Toby and Sir Andrew that they must be quiet.

As I descended the stairs and walked down the hall, the noise from their caterwauling was as absonant as the din of wild boars scuffling over a truffle patch. Presenting song, Sir Toby bellowed out, "On the twelfth day of Christmas …"

Mariah, having arrived on the scene just before me, bade him to keep the peace.

I addressed them directly. "My masters, are you

mad? Have you no wit, manners, nor honesty but to gabble like tinkers at this time of night? Do you make an alehouse of my lady's house that you squawk out your awful harmony without any mitigation or remorse of voice? Is there no respect of place, persons, nor time in you?" The house was in mourning, they well knew.

Sir Toby had a flimsy reply about respecting time in their singing. *What an arrogant upper-class oaf! God send us better companions.*

"Sir Toby, I must be round with you," I replied. "My lady bade me tell you that, though she harbors you as her kinsman, she's not allied to your disorders. If you can separate yourself and your misdemeanors, you are welcome to the house; if not, and if it would please you to take leave of her, she is very willing to bid you farewell." These were my lady's thoughts, though not her exact words. After a few moments, Sir Toby must have reckoned I was overstating my instructions. He was still drunk, still swaggering and singing—assisted by Feste, Sir Andrew, and, to some extent, Mariah.

"Art thou any more than a steward?" He slobbered at me, thick in tongue. "Dost thou think, because thou art virtuous, there shall be no more cakes and ale?" He told me to go rub my steward's chain with crumbs, and then he demanded more wine from Mariah.

Sir Toby is out of bounds in this mourning house, but I do not rule my lady's noble kinsmen. The servants, however, are a different matter.

"Mistress Mariah, if you prized my lady's favor at anything more than contempt, you would not give means for this uncivil rule." I told her I would report it to my lady. Then I removed myself from confrontation, having relayed my lady's wishes, but I lingered in the hall to listen.

"Go shake your ears," Mariah blatted. The little aspiring hypocrite would not have the nerve to say that to my face, although soon enough she would make me an ass. As a woman scorned, she had bided time for her fury.

I am a bachelor, alone in my apartments. Some months ago, I was a fool for Mariah's love. I returned her advances, and we became intimate. I thought we would marry, but I discovered her grunting astride a delivering tradesman. That's all one, and we are done. Now she sets her sights higher and stalks Sir Toby. I marvel at my former attention to this small, spiteful wren. In many ways, she is an adept wench, and I had reason to bear in mind her harbored resentment. She acted as if the rejection were my fault and set upon so mean a reprisal as only one who knows you intimately can devise. She found my Achilles' heel, a weakness, a vulnerability, where she could work her vengeance.

To this enterprise, Mariah recruited Sir Toby, Sir Andrew, and two other roguish betrayers, Feste and Fabian. Fabian is a rough laborer once favored by my lady for moving rosebushes and grooming her favorite horse. The aspirer has learned to read and looks for higher station, but I have called him out as a woodcock poacher and an attender of bear baitings.

"I would rather be boiled in melancholy than miss

a chance to get back at him," Fabian has told others. He blames me, not his own actions, for his loss of favor.

During this sad period, I had become more familiar to my lady, young as she is. I became her closest confidant. She sought my counsel and treated me fair above all others in all-important events, and socially as well. She said to me once that she "would fancy a man of my complexion," and I gave her my best efforts always. It is my grievous fault that I cannot interpret whether a woman is fawning favor in exchange or is inviting amorous attention. I remark that, with many women, it looks exactly the same.

I don't know when I began to imagine that Olivia might love me. Perhaps it was after her many rebuffs of Duke Orsino. "I cannot love him," she told Cesario. "Let him send no more." Her loneliness without her father and brother raised my feelings for her, as well. I wanted to protect her, and certainly the estate would flourish in my permanent reign.

I discovered a letter in the garden on my usual walking path. It seemed to have been left for me. I know now that it was the forging Mariah who served this little dish of poison. By my very life, the letter appeared to be my lady's hand. It began, "To the unknown beloved, this and my good wishes." It seemed Olivia's very phrases! But it was the soft wax and the impression of my lady's seal that won me over, liver and all.

The letter ended, "If this falls into thy hand, resolve. In my stars I am above thee; but be not afraid of greatness: some are born great, some achieve greatness, and some have greatness thrust upon them." (Rousing words! Who would guess these were merely part of an elaborate hoax?) The letter further said I should present myself smiling and in yellow stockings, cross-gartered, as an indication of my acceptance of this offered love. It was signed with the oxymoron, "The Fortunate-Unhappy."

My love, hopes, dreams, and especially my vanity caught me. I was certain that my fortunate lady loved me. I would smile and show my legs cross-gartered and in yellow. I praised Jove for raising my stars. I would make her happy.

Mariah had set the stage for my downfall at court. When I came to my lady, the countess had been told to expect a strange, mad Malvolio, a man out of keeping with the mourning house, one who appeared as a smiling, overweening, yellow-stockinged clown. Oh, how ludicrous. In hindsight, even I must laugh.

"How now, Malvolio!" The countess said when I came to her in the formal garden with Mariah present.

"Sweet lady, ho, ho." My face ached with the broad sustainment of my beaming grin.

"Smilest thou? I sent for thee upon a sad occasion." She was dressed in black, veil raised to greet me. I told her I could be sad with the cross-gartered obstruction of the blood, but that I recognized her sweet Roman hand.

"Wilt thou go to bed, Malvolio?" My lady suggested. I took this the wrong way.

"To bed! Ay, sweetheart, and I'll come to thee." Bed with my lovely lady. Oh!

"God comfort thee!" She said. I blush in shame as I recall the scene.

Then Mariah started, "Why appear you with this ridiculous boldness before my lady?" I recounted to my lady with a wink, "'Be not afraid of greatness.' 'Twas well writ."

"What meanest thou by that, Malvolio?" My lady replied.

"'Some are born great,'"

"Ha!"

"'Some achieve greatness,'"

"What sayest thou?"

"'And some have greatness *thrust* upon them.'" I said this with my hips as well.

"Heaven restore thee!"

"Remember who commended my yellow stockings,"

"Thy yellow stockings!" She raised her hands to the sides of her head.

"And wished to see me cross-gartered."

"Cross-gartered!"

At this point a servant approached and announced the reappearance of Cesario, who with his usual insistence, demanded immediate audience. The doorman noted that he could hardly entreat him back. I was surprised that my lady said she would go to him, instead of him to her. She gave instructions to Mariah that I should be looked to by Toby and other persons, calling me "fellow."

"I would not have him miscarry for the half of my dowry," she said. I know now that she meant she worried for me only as her valued steward.

Sir Toby, Mariah, and Fabian, with their henchmen, did not take long to exploit this. My lady was already in the belief that I was mad. With rough servants from the stable, they had me bound, carried off, and put in a dark cell with a small, barred window. They carried this uncivil prank, for their pleasure and my penance, till their very pastime prompted them to have mercy on me. But first they wanted fun.

Mariah and Sir Toby enlisted Feste to approach me in disguise. She prepared a gown and false beard so that he could present himself to me as Sir Topas, the curate. Within my imprisoned hearing, Sir Toby and Feste carried on a conversation to lead me to believe the fiction.

"Jove bless thee, master Parson," I heard Sir Toby say.

"*Bonos dies*, Sir Toby," Feste greeted in Latin, "for, as the old hermit of Prague that never saw pen and ink very wittily said to a niece of the king, 'That that is, is'; so I, being Master Parson, am Master Parson, for what is 'that' but 'that,' and 'is' but 'is'?"

Perhaps there are places where the meaning of the word "is" is not debated. Here in Illyria anything goes, but I thought these statements a strange greeting. I was confused.

"To him, Sir Topas," Sir Toby said, directing Feste to my window.

"What, ho, I say! Peace in this prison!" Feste, as Sir Topas, said to me.

I asked from within, "Who calls there?" I was never able to see Feste's face, and he is a well-counterfeiting knave.

Feste answered, "Sir Topas, the curate, who comes to visit Malvolio, the lunatic."

"Sir Topas, Sir Topas, good Sir Topas, go to my lady."

"Out, hyperbolical fiend! How vexest thou this man! Talkest thou of nothing but ladies?"

"Well said, Master Parson. Sir Topas, never was man thus wronged. Good Sir Topas, do not think I am mad. They have laid me here in hideous darkness."

"Fie, thou dishonest Satan! I call thee by the most modest terms; for I am one of those gentle ones that will use the devil himself with courtesy; sayest thou that your house is dark?"

"I am not mad, Sir Topas; I say to you, this house is dark."

"Madman, thou errest; I say, there is no darkness but ignorance, in which thou art more puzzled than the Egyptians in their fog."

I should have recognized his overacting. *What a cardenio!* He engaged me in more debate for his pleasure, warning me of moral pugnacity. *The nerve!* Under great duress, I struggled in that hole to retain my dignity.

In this gross humiliation, I hold my deepest resentment for Feste. It was he who serendipitously found me in disadvantage. He used this opportunity to try to drive me from a supposed madman to a real one. It was he who put on the disguise. It was he who deepened my despair and tried to upset my mind.

It was an act so severe that even Sir Toby began to blanch at its implement. Sir Toby assessed how my lady would perceive the offense, and he must have pondered the effect it might have on Mariah's situation. Still, Sir Toby could not resist setting up more sport. As instructed by Sir Toby, Feste returned to me as himself, singing, "Hey, Robin, jolly Robin. Tell me how thy lady does."

"Fool!" I shouted. Here was my rescue. He kept singing. I called again. "Good fool, as ever thou wilt deserve well at my hand, help me to a candle and pen and ink and paper. As I am a gentleman, I will live to be thankful to thee for it."

"Master Malvolio?" He finally answered.

"Ay, good fool."

"Alas, sir, how fell you beside your five wits?"

"Fool, there was never a man so notoriously abused: I am as well in my wits, fool, as thou art."

"But as well? Then you are mad indeed, if you be no better in your wits than a fool." He was really giving it to me.

"They have here imprisoned me, kept me in darkness, and sent ministers to me, such asses. And they have done all they can to force me out of my wits."

"Careful what you say. The minister is here."

He knew I could not see him from my darkness, so he began to speak to me in changing voices, as Sir Topas and himself.

"Malvolio, thy wits the heavens restore! Endeavor thyself to sleep, and leave thy vain bibble-babble."

"Sir Topas!" I said.

(As Sir Topas) "Maintain no words with him, good fellow." (As Feste) "Who, I, sir?" (As Sir Topas) "Not I, sir." (As Feste) "God be with you, good Sir Topas." (As Sir Topas) "Merry, amen." (As Feste) "I will, sir, I will."

What good sport he had, shifting from voice to voice. "Fool, fool, I say!" I entreated him to bring me paper, pen, and ink to write my lady.

The clown left, singing, "I am gone, sir. And anon, sir," and more such drivel. Later he returned with what I asked, waited while I wrote, and departed with my letter. This allowance was largely at Sir Toby's urging, I am sure. Sir Toby had become worried.

There were major events outside my presence, especially when Cesario's twin brother, Sebastian, turned up. Olivia and Sebastian, who presented a handsomer version of the slightly effeminate Cesario, fell in love at an unnatural rate. They were both in need of the other, and the wooing had been accomplished by Cesario. Olivia insisted she and Sebastian be married immediately. Sebastian must have thought he had died and gone to heaven when he had found the beautiful and rich countess so dedicated to him.

I am told there was some swordplay between Sir Toby and Sebastian, with Olivia intervening and calling Sir Toby an ungrateful wretch "fit for the mountains and the barbarous caves."

It got even zanier. Cesario was wondrously revealed

as the feminine Viola. Letting down her hair, she made explanations to all. As a shipwrecked orphan who had no one to protect her, she decided to disguise herself as a young man so that she would have a man's freedom to move about. She enlisted the captain to help her in this falsehood, and she had the talent to make the pretense good

Orsino, the big fool in love with love, immediately transferred his affections for Olivia to the clever Viola. The meaning of her vows of love became clear to him. How quickly the love's plague can be passed around. Viola had wooed Olivia for Sebastian, and Orsino for himself—err … herself.

Upon Viola's revelation my release was begun. They wanted to know why the captain, who befriended Viola, was being held. It was only then that Feste produced my letter.

For fear of punishment, he delayed deliverance until this moment, and he tried to suggest the letter was no matter, saying, "Look then to be well edified when the fool delivers the madman." Feste, the illiterate, still jesting, read it as bibble-babble, so my lady made Fabian read it to all.

"By the Lord, madam, you wrong me, and the world shall know it: though you have put me into darkness and given your drunken cousin rule over me, yet I have the benefit of my senses as well as your ladyship. I have your own letter that induced me to the semblance I put on. I speak out of my injury." I had signed it "The Madly-Used Malvolio."

My lady immediately had me released and brought to her. I arrived still dirty from my imprisonment. "Madam, you have done me wrong, notorious wrong."

"Have I, Malvolio? No."

"Lady, you have. Pray you, peruse that letter." I gave her the note from the path. "You must not now deny it is your hand. Or say 'tis not your seal, nor your invention." I began pleading. "And why have you suffered me to be imprisoned, kept in a dark house, visited by the priest, and made the most notorious geck and gull that e'er invention played on? Tell me why."

"Alas, Malvolio, this is not my writing, though, I confess, much like the character, but out of question 'tis Mariah's hand. And now I recall, it was she first told me thou was't mad. This practice hath most shrewdly passed upon thee, but when we know the grounds and authors of it, thou shalt be both the plaintiff and the judge of thine own cause."

Then Fabian's guilt overcame him. "Most freely I confess. Myself and Toby set this device against Malvolio here. Mariah wrote the letter at Sir Toby's great urging. In recompense whereof he hath married her."

Turning to me, Olivia said, "Alas, poor fool, how have they baffled thee!"

Feste began to mock me. "Why, 'Some are born great, some achieve greatness, and some have greatness thrown upon them.' I was one, sir, in this interlude; one Sir Topas, sir. But do you remember? 'Madam, why laugh you at such a barren rascal? You smile not, and he is gagged.' And thus the whirligig of time brings in its revenges."

"I'll be revenged on the whole pack of you," I shouted, exiting in my shame.

As I recovered, I strengthened and consolidated my standing with the count and countess. I apologized for my foolishness, and they forgave me. They have agreed with me that an attack on their steward was an attack on the estate and to their very authority. My best revenge has been to make the estate hum with efficiency. None hinder my undertakings, unlike before.

"For these results, I give you many thanks, Malvolio," Count Sebastian said. "Our estate may be the finest in Illyria."

For Sir Toby and his Dame Mariah, their own actions sealed their fate. Although she attracted him and he acquired love's local plague, he also was obliged to marry her. I would have had her sacked as the author of this malignant jest. Mariah will have her hands full with the alcoholic, dependent, and unemployable Sir Toby. Someday she'll need work again. I will see that the reference she receives will be no better than it should be.

Sir Toby will not be welcome soon again in this household, if ever. You may remember that he and Sebastian had an altercation. My masters agree with me that it would be very awkward to receive Sir Toby and his new bride, the former attendant to my lady. The bills Sir Toby and Sir Andrew ran up in their long stay here were high as Vesuvius, and my lady and my lord were astonished at the sums. At my suggestion, they reduced Sir Toby's support from the family estate by half for recompense.

Fabian has been conscripted into the army, which suddenly recognized his many skills.

Feste travels much for a jester. He has served many years in this household, but he has grown tired of his lot. I have found that he has accounts in the next town—overly large amounts for someone called fool. He juggles in jail while my friend the sheriff completes his inquiries. My lady will have no more of him.

As for the countess, leave her to heaven, and to Sebastian. While her ambivalence gave me expectations, I let myself go off too far. She had no hand in these ill devices.

Revenge is disappointing. I had hoped for a sweet magnum of satisfaction, but in some ways, I would rather turn back the clock. My affected superiority invited mischief. If I had credited others with more worth, they would have not so happily conspired against me. Still, I am not too old to transfigure. I will take an offered job with the Duke Orsino and his true Duchess Viola. It provides a higher salary and greater staff in a finer household. I will be the maestro of his estates, organize his household, and help him manage his followers.

Of the twins, the duke got the better of the pair. Viola's love labor won both matches. My Lady Olivia benefits. She is not suited for a single life devoted to her estate. If Sebastian be like his sister, the countess has a good man. Olivia and Orsino were too much alike, needing others to provide their entertainment and actions. The twins will provide the zest to their individual marriages.

Now we return to our beginning question: Why should I be the dunce of this Twelfth Night? So many have fallen for love's honeyed tricks: Olivia, Sebastian, Toby, Mariah, Andrew, Orsino, and Viola. Was I more ridiculous than the others? I think only nobles will be saved the indignities and consequences of absurd love. My masters are still so young and play at foolish things. They fail to see through the wind and the rain, while we hardworking followers must strive to please them every day.

Back to Sleep

"It's almost seven thirty. What are you still doing in the bedroom?" Lisa, my tall, brunette late thirties wife calls down the hall from the living room.

"Rolling socks," I answer, sitting on the side of the bed, trying to wake up. The socks thing is a reference to yesterday's argument. I don't mind doing laundry because she needs more time to study, but I refuse to roll socks. Life is short.

"Sarcasm isn't your forte."

"I'm better with irony." Actually, I'm pretty good with sarcasm, but when you're married, you have to lay off. "I'm up. Getting ready. Don't have a fit."

My no-longer-needed alarm sounds, and I hit the off button quickly.

Beep, beep, bee—

Went to bed late last night, still a little fuzzy. Rubbing my eyes, I shuffle toward the master bathroom and announce, "I got the shower. I'll be out in a couple of minutes." Lisa doesn't need to get in here; she is mostly ready and drinking coffee.

The family is headed for the early church service at nine. It's a rarity that we, Brian and Lisa Hall with daughter Olivia, attend the early service. This is laid-back California, and I like to sleep in on the weekends, and so does the fifteen-year-old Olivia. Lisa, however, has gone over to the bright side. When we met in college, we were both night owls, but as a working mother, she reverted to the more practical parenting schedule. Going to bed early versus staying up until midnight has been a source of conflict between us.

Last night, I got her out to the late movie. When Lisa has the time—this is her spring break—it usually has to be the early movie. But dinner at a restaurant started late because of Olivia's afternoon soccer game in another town. Upon getting home from the theater about midnight, Lisa went straight to bed. I stayed up to watch some of *The English Patient* with Ralph Fiennes and Kristin Scott Thomas, drank a beer, and then slept like a rock until about five, when I became restless.

With Lisa's mother-teacher-student schedule, we don't go to church every Sunday, but we attend frequently, almost always to the main service. Even a night owl can drag himself out of bed by nine or so to get to church by ten thirty. Post-Easter on this warm spring morning, the early service would still draw forty to fifty worshippers. It is held in the small chapel on the other side of the Sunday school classrooms.

No matter which service we attend, we practice just-in-time delivery. Depositing Olivia in simultaneous Sunday School Youth Group at our church near Benicia, we are never quite late, but sometimes we're ushered down the aisle only moments before the choir files in singing the first hymn. Today we are early for the early service because Olivia is playing her music festival flute solo. She will play during the collection, entertaining while the plates are passed. At the main service, the choir will sing at this interval.

When we arrive at the church, out of habit, the three of us hurry from the parking lot into the church and down the hall to the chapel. You can't get into the chapel without passing through a gauntlet of greeters with their outstretched hands. The couple assigned as official greeters were stationed in the chapel foyer, shaking the hands of all entrants, saying good morning with cheesy smiles. Today the line started with a white-haired, businesslike, female lay liturgist, whose name tag I can't read, and Reverend Paul, our senior minister, in full robe and regalia. I dutifully shake each hand presented. The reverend's hand pops out like a snapping turtle, grasping my larger hand with his strong thumb, short of a full grip.

"Good morning. Peace be with you."

"Good morning. With you as well," I say.

Reverend Paul is a large-voiced, rotund, ostensibly wise man, about fifty. The eventual theme of each of his sermons is the same: Have faith in Jesus and everything will be all right. I have never heard him elevate to consider justice, truth, and beauty in the modern context, but perhaps I'm asking too much. The reverend's grip is off, strong and then weak. Also, something in the reverend's expression gives me a funny feeling. As he releases my hand, I'm certain that something peculiar has crossed his mind. Reverend Paul's look is not reproachful. It is questioning, as if, upon seeing me, he has a new variable to consider. *An odd look from a cleric. Curiouser and curiouser.* I let it go and walk into the chapel. Still, I have an odd feeling.

"Let's sit down in front on the left," Lisa suggests.

"Okay. There's always room down in front." Mother and Father will have a good view of daughter playing her solo.

The service starts with the congregation singing one hymn, accompanied by the organist, then a few words by the liturgist, and then a recitation in unison from the printed program. I yawn through the announcements. It's the usual format, comfortable and familiar. I examine the dull shine on my shoes and the design of the carpet on the floor.

Reverend Paul gives us a long prayer—warming up for his sermon, I suppose. Getting drowsy, I fear that if I keep my eyes closed during all of the prayer, I will fall fast asleep. Toward the end, he thanks God for the good weather and, apparently assuming God is a baseball fan, asks that it continue through tomorrow for the Giants' opening day.

When Reverend Paul starts the sermon, my thoughts are elsewhere. I'm more than half dozing, eyes barely open, face directed left out the floor-to-ceiling window of the chapel to a formal garden. *Too warm in here; the room is kept too warm. It's for the old people lacking good blood circulation.* I gaze out the window and nod at a brown-headed Steller's jay that hops on a bush limb and peers in at me.

After a while, the minister's words begin to override my drowsy interest in the spring scene outside. I hear words like "promiscuity," "infidelity," and "adultery." The words aren't shouted. They aren't even said in the same sentence. They are part of the sermon. Usually, his sermons are about the Bible and faith—standard stuff, easy listening. Refocusing, I look up at Reverend Paul. From my low vantage point, I see that he and the liturgist, seated now, are looking right down at me! Why? Their attention is startling. I don't get it for several seconds. *The bastard! Don't panic.* Ministers tell stories about men flinching when the annual sermon about adultery is read out. Guilt makes them squirm for their wife and all others to see. *Apparently, Reverend Paul has decided that if there is an adulterer in this small group, I am it.* I appear to be the youngest adult male in the chapel—although I'm beginning middle age. It's a slow league for prospective adulterers. I imagine that even if there were adulterers in the congregation, most of these fornicators, being night persons, would attend the late service.

"To keep thee from the evil woman and from the flattery of the tongue of a strange woman." Reverend Paul says he is quoting Proverbs 6. "Lust not after her beauty in thine heart; neither let her take thee with her eyelids," the reverend continues.

Oh, fuck. Anna's beauty in my heart! I don't need this.

I have control. Why worry about it now? Keep calm; don't blush for the reverend.

Anna, the tall, cute, sweet, and blonde divorcée who worked for me at the Riverside Center, is some twenty years my junior. It blew me away when she started looking at me as though I were the coolest guy on earth. Her big eyes widened, and she seemed to hang on my every syllable. I had never been so flattered. It was overwhelming, like a tsunami washing me off my foundations.

She worked out every day and looked like a cheerleader—such a tight little butt. She had a slightly chipped tooth, which the office insurance would have fixed, that made her all the more endearing. For a while I basked in her attentions, and it started rumors. I walked down to her office and talked and flirted with her. Stood in her doorway. At last year's office Christmas party, when Lisa didn't come, I spent most of the party with her. Didn't take her home. But I began to think of her and her young body almost constantly. Previously, I had always been immune to the attentions of other women, but a combination of events broke down my resistance like a virus.

Lisa teaches high school full-time and is going to law school. She preps for her job and grades papers; then she is either gone to class or taking the online courses, which are up 24-7. There is no time for other things, and she is mostly oblivious to my life. I cook or pick up most of the weekday dinners. We have a cleaning lady, but I do most of the laundry and all the driving to teenage appointments. When Lisa converses, it is always about the men she goes to law school with, and especially about Jim, who is in her carpool. The carpool often gets home late. Sometimes she and Jim and others make Saturday trips to the law library together. Feeling guilty for not being there for me, she is often defensively curt as well.

Anna was so sweet. She melted through my defenses. The relatively short period of my infatuation has been the only time I had wanted another woman. I fantasized for months but never actually did anything. I never touched her, except in a slow dance. I never met her anywhere, never suggested anything—probably because, in the end, I really didn't want to. Or was I just chicken? But fate had intervened, anyway.

"We need you to take over the Concord area office," my boss told me out of the blue. "It's a little closer to your home, and we have a small raise."

With mixed feelings, I took the transfer to some degree because I thought my boss was trying to save my ass, and it was getting embarrassing. Almost immediately, my obsession with Anna dulled. I made up business reasons to call her a couple of times, but I have not seen her again after saying good-bye to the whole office. I was taken aback when she married a man her own age just three months later, and I've heard that she has given her notice. She is leaving for a job nearer where her husband works down near San Jose. I'm glad for her, and relieved ... and slightly disappointed. Sometimes I miss the excitement of my obsession, short as it was. On the whole, though, it makes me feel silly. Another lesson has come to me as well—understanding. I now understand how things can get started. How easily one could turn down that path.

"Can a man take fire in his bosom and his clothes not be burned?" Reverend Paul was still with the proverbs. *Maybe just singed*, I thought. As for feeling especially guilty over small potatoes before the reverend in the middle of the early service, I think I should be culpable for acts, not thoughts. Nevertheless, I'm facing a practical problem. Whatever the actual condition of my conscience, if I look nervous, I'll look guilty— guilty to the reverend, the liturgist, the congregation, and worst of all, to my wife next to me and even to my daughter. *Is anyone picking up this little drama?*

I yawn and blink twice. *Go with it.* I look out the window again and watch the jay and the sparrows dart among the bushes. *Don't care what the reverend thinks. Ministers' opinions are unimportant. Is he disappointed in my nonreaction? Does he think I'm acting, successfully covering my guilt? He doesn't appear to be monitoring anyone else's demeanor, damn it.* The reverend may resent that I was not a strong churchman. One of my irreverent observations may have returned to haunt me. Perhaps the reverend hoped I would be bothered by the sermon. Maybe he even chose it because he knew I would be coming today to hear my daughter play. *No, that's paranoid. Back to sleep. It is not a concern.* I'm mature enough not to conjure up and magnify atrophying guilt feelings. Nodding at the window, feeling torpid and content, I'm slipping into semiconsciousness. Wait!

Along my back, from one side to the other, I feel something warm and soft. Lisa has slipped her arm around me along the top of the pew. *Well this is a new twist.* I wear the arm graciously, like a newly bestowed award. *But what the hell is Lisa trying to say? Has she also been monitoring my reactions?* Apparently, I have passed the test. Is she demonstrating her faith in me as a husband? Is it approval for this honest sleepiness?

Don't overreact.

Reverend Paul has stopped droning about sexual hedonism and is moving on to his reoccurring central theme: Having faith in Jesus will turn it all around and make everything Okay. *Back to sleep.* Dozing snugly under my wife's protection, I see the reverend has quit looking at me. Half-watching with drooping eyelids through the sunny window, I relax while the birds are joined by a squirrel.

Rest up for the flute solo.

Printed in the United States
By Bookmasters